The Great Disappointment

A Confession

by

Susan Taylor Chehak

FOREVERLAND PRESS
Silverthorne, Colorado
http://www.foreverlandpress.com

Cover and Book Design
by http:/ebooklaunch.com

Critical acclaim for the work of

Susan Taylor Chehak

SMITHEREENS

"Dark, disturbing and compelling, this is an astonishing read that shouldn't be missed." —*Company* (England)

RAMPAGE

"Chehak's darkly evocative midwestern gothic is a stunning exploration of love, lust, greed, envy, innocence, murder, and obsession. Unforgettable characters, a grim and riveting plot, and darkly lyrical prose add up to great reading." —*Booklist*

DANCING ON GLASS

"A deeply chilling, disturbing, beautifully written novel. Shocking, stunningly written... Faulkner himself would have admired and respected [DANCING ON GLASS]... Its events should linger in the reader's mind long after it has been read."—*Los Angeles Daily News*

HARMONY

"A gifted author... this enigmatic, tantalizing, beautifully underwritten tale is less reminiscent of other contemporary thrillers than of novels by Ford Madox Ford and John Hawkes."—*The Kirkus Reviews*

THE STORY OF ANNIE D.

"Absolutely stunning... Reads with the force and generational sweep of some ancient rural myth. Like the author, Annie D. is such a mesmerizing storyteller that you can almost feel the fire at your back." —*The New York Times Book Review*

For Tom

Everything you can think of is true. —Tom Waits

Let the people who never find true love
keep saying that there's no such thing. —Wislawa Szymborska

Chapter One

How about if, for now, we skip the once upon a time? That, and who she was and where she was born, how she grew up with her mom (accountant) and her dad (actuary) in a world of numbers and dates and formulas and facts with one living sister (Janet, seven years older) and one dead brother (Horace, the infamous unborn twin) in a smallish brick house in Nowhere, New York, with trees in the yard (maple and oak) and bushes by the windows (juniper) and flowers in the garden (roses, lilies, irises) and one of those quilted covers over the toaster that matched the oven mitts above the stove—just to give you a fee-ling for Mrs. Mifflin and her sense of style (toilet seat covers, refrigerator magnets, pastel sweater sets, sensi-ble shoes). How about instead we go right to the point where she found herself at the end of this story, all out of options with nowhere to turn because she'd alre-ady done everything that she could think to do to put things right again when they had all gone so terribly, and to her mind tragically, wrong?

Which was: holed up in the English Department offices on the third floor of Stanley Hall at Springer College in Brevity, Iowa—*Veritas Odit Moras*—with the triple loop of a fully loaded Ping-Pong ball bomb collar around her neck like a string of oversized pearls on a little girl playing pretend, which is pretty much what she was. Except that this was not a game, it was real. One flick of the Bic and ka-boom.

What else do you want to know?

Her name was Mollie Mifflin, and maybe you've already heard of her, because she did gain some notoriety after what happened, but it's important to understand that before that she was no one. She was 17 years old at the time of her crime—if it was a crime, and that's still up for debate—and she had never been in any kind of trouble before. That's not to say she wasn't everything her mother always believed her to be, which was a liar and, now and then, a thief. Maybe it's just to say that she'd never been caught.

We can tell you this: she sincerely didn't mean for it to go as far as it did. She had always hoped that someday she'd be famous (doesn't everybody?), that she'd do something big, something important, something that would make people sit up and pay attention. That she'd be someone, somehow, and yet never in the wildest of her wild dreams did she ever imagine that it would have come to the crisis that it did and become the legend that it has. But there it is. The truth won't wait.

The facts as we know them are these: a certain Ms. Mollie Mifflin was in the employ of Mr. and Mrs. Deacon Bensenhaver Molene at the time of what everybody thought and said was their collapse. She'd been working for them for about three months by then, since the start of summer. Job title? Housekeeper. Caretaker. Companion. Job description? Do whatever there was that needed doing. Cooking, cleaning, shopping, washing, mending, minding. You name it, and it was Mollie's to do for them.

The arrangement that they had was not exactly a formal one, because that's not how it happened. And it wasn't something that she was trained to do, either—she would be the first to admit that. Quite the opposite. If Mollie was trained to do anything, it was to keep to herself and stay out of the way, not be the one whose responsibility it was to get everything done to make sure that somebody else was fed and warm and clean and dry (and safe and sound and whatnot).

She was nobody's mother (yet), and she was not a nurse, either. There is no evidence to suggest that she ever explicitly claimed that to be her profession, to the Molenes or to anybody else, although it's possible that some assumptions were made and then left to stand, without any denial or correction from her. She did wear a uniform sometimes—that's been documented—so maybe this made it seem like the position was more legitimate than it actually was? Or maybe it made it seem like she was pretending to be someone that she was not.

That white nurse's uniform (skirt, blouse, stockings, shoes) was all her own doing. She has admitted to that, too. Nobody asked her to wear it. Nobody told her to wear it. This was all Mollie's own personal choice, of her own personal devising.

At one point she found herself wanting to show it to her mother, but that was clearly just wishful thinking, and besides, Mollie was not about to spend the money to call and say, "Hey, Mom! I have a job and I wear a uniform and I know what I'm doing and people trust me!" because she knew her mother would not get it, and even if she did she wouldn't have cared, not really. Or worse, she wouldn't have believed it anyway. Nevertheless, the uniform did mean something to Mollie, which maybe makes it sound more complicated than it was. She just liked the phony white fabric. She liked how it was clean and slick and easy to take care of, too. Wash warm. Drip dry. Cool iron, if you must. It was important-looking. Seriou-s-seeming. And if you want to know the truth, she liked how it looked on her. She has always had a classic figure. Very small waist. Long legs. Full hips. Nice breasts. Emily had been heard to say more than once that to her Mollie was the very picture of an angel.

She bought the whites at the Green Square Swap Meet that they have in downtown Brevity every Sunday in summer. On her days off, Mollie prowled the church bazaars and tag sales around town. Because Number One, she was a frugal person (thanks, Mom) and Number Two, she knew a good bargain when she saw it (thanks, Dad), she was able to outfit herself quite well while she was in Brevity, and nobody was the wiser. Plus, Number Three, Mollie had no living expenses to speak of at that time (thanks, nobody but herself). She worked hard to pay her way. She did what she had to do, that's all.

Mollie was not able to tell anyone where the woman who sold those uniforms to her got them for herself because the fact is: she never asked about it. For all Mollie knew, they weren't even hers in the first place. Or if they were, she had definitely grown out of them and probably so some time ago. Maybe the woman used to be a nurse herself, when she was younger, or thinner. Or maybe she had a daughter who had been a nurse and then she died of something that she picked up from one of her patients and now the mom was trying to get rid of her daughter's old stuff, for which she had no use anymore, and make a little bit of money from it at the same time. To pay for the casket and the funeral and the flowers and so on and so forth and all like that. That whole train of thought brings up some other questions, though, ones that may or may not be important. Such as: Are nurses allowed to sell their old uniforms? And: Is wearing a nurse's uniform some kind of an impersonation? And: Could a person get in trouble for impersonating a nurse? If so, it probably doesn't matter anyway because that's definitely not the worst thing that Mollie has ever done, before or since.

The Molenes weren't looking for help when Mollie showed up. In fact, they didn't even know they needed it until there she was, emerging from the mist, an apparition at their door, hungry and cold, because she'd been on the road for several days already by then, riding on the Greyhound from Erie to Ottumwa, with a hitchhike at either end and three stopovers along the way.

Mollie's thought was that Emily would take one look and know how much she loved her, she'd be so happy to see her, she'd take her in without a moment's hesitation, and then they'd have this perfect little family, the family of Mollie's dreams. Maybe there would even be other kids, Emily's own children, a bunch of brothers and sisters for her to have to contend with. They'd be jealous at first, but then when they got to know Mollie better, they'd realize that she was no threat to anything, and then they'd come to count her as one of their own. By the time she actually got there, however, it was way too late for any of that. A lifetime too late. Too much time had passed already, and Mollie was too young and Emily was too old. Deek, too. Besides, there weren't any children anyway. Never had been.

Mollie tried. She did the best she knew how. But it was impossible, and before she knew it, the whole thing had just gone too far. That was not her fault. (We must insist upon this.)

It was early summer when Mollie arrived, and a storm had rolled in over the plains on its way to the mountains far away, so it was raining—the kind of blind, solid downpour that stops just as suddenly as it starts—and she was soaked. In fact, she was a mess in all kinds of ways at that time. A rag, a bone, a hank of hair, as her Aunt Lucy had been heard to say. Of herself, of course, not of Mollie.

She had hitched from Nowhere to Erie, in the dark and all alone, just a girl, with nothing but her own wits to keep her safe from harm. A nice woman in a family van stopped and offered her a ride and then turned around and scolded her for accepting it, going on about how she used to bum rides when she was in college but that was then and this is now and you can't trust anybody anymore (though it seemed she was having no problem trusting Mollie), until finally she let Mollie out at the bus station with another warning to be careful and pay attention and don't talk to anybody, especially not if he's a man. Either it was awhile before this lady missed the two 20-dollar bills from the wallet in her purse, or she didn't want to admit to her own vulnerability, because Mollie never saw her again, although she did spend four more hours at the station waiting for the bus to come in. By the time she'd begun to feel the stab of remorse and think about somehow giving the money back, Mollie was long gone, and it was too late for any of that. By then, it was the middle of the night and so far away from Nowhere that Mollie didn't even know where she was anymore. More no one and nowhere than she'd ever been before. She half expected that her family might be looking for her, that her mother would be sorry when she saw that Mollie had left not just her house, but the town altogether, but that didn't happen (more wishful thinking), so it looked like Mrs. Mifflin was as glad as she had always told her younger daughter she would be that the girl was gone and out of her hair.

Mostly it was uneventful, but the one good thing that occurred on that trip was that Mollie experienced her first real mind-reading episode—after all those fruitless months of lessons and hard work and practice at it—and when it finally happened, she realized that she'd been doing it all wrong, all along. She had been calling it mind reading, but that was a total misnomer, misleading in its implication that what she was supposed to do was use her intuition to read other people's minds and so that way she could come to know what they were thinking. You see, she thought if she could learn to do that, then she would know just what they wanted, and then maybe she could find a way to give it to them somehow, whatever it was—if it wasn't too expensive, that is, and if it wasn't something that would bring misery to someone else—and then they would be happy. This was how Mollie Mifflin was going to save the world. She figured the more people who were happy, the fewer people who would be unhappy, not only because their own minds had been changed but also because that made them nicer to everyone else around them. Like a virus, she thought, such happiness couldn't help but spread. (Naïve girl. Such a child. If nothing else, we have to love her for that.)

But what Mollie learned, there in the dark on that bus on a highway from Nowhere into nowhere, was that she wasn't the one who was supposed to read other people's thoughts; it was other people who were supposed to read hers by her sending them out strong enough and in just the right way so that the other person would be able to hear it and pick it up. It wasn't clear what good that did them, whether it would make anybody any happier if only they could know what Mollie was thinking, unless what she was thinking was about how good and beautiful and perfect they were—which was, most of the time, a big enough challenge in itself, nevermind sending such thoughts out loud and strong enough that they might have a chance of being overheard. No wonder it was so hard.

You know when you stare at the back of someone's head and then eventually they snap to and turn around and look at you? Like that. Or when you're thinking about someone you haven't thought about for a long time and then all of a sudden the phone rings and there they are, telling you that they've been thinking about you, too. It wasn't mind *reading* that was Mollie's psychic talent. It was mind *writing*. Or to put it another way, it was mind control.

This was a tremendous revelation to our girl. So huge it almost made her turn around and go back home to try again. Because once she had it figured out, well, that changed everything. Once she knew what she was supposed to do, then she also knew what she was going to have to do to practice getting better at it.

The mind belonged to an endomorph. Female, maybe 40 years old, black hair, blue eyes, medium height, 250 pounds and all that goes with that—shortness of breath, diabetes, high blood pressure, varicose veins inking the insides of her thighs. She had taken the aisle seat next to Mollie, who honestly had no prejudice against her for her size, per se. Mrs. Mifflin happened to be a fat woman, too, and Mollie's sister and her aunt Lucy—those three of the most important women in her life, all of them were overweight in their own way. No, it was that she was taking up more than her fair share of the seating area and her skin was deathly white and, where it touched Mollie's, clammy and cold. Soon she was sleeping. Mollie stared at her. She thought daggers: "Go away. Go away. Go away.

You don't want to sit next to me. You don't want to be here." And then, two hundred miles later, at the next stop, the woman woke up and she got off, just like that. So maybe that proves something. Whether you think so or not, the point is, Mollie believed it did.

We might wonder what Emily Molene must have thought when she saw Mollie that first night after she arrived in Brevity, and we might reasonably guess that she was scared. Even after Mollie explained to her who she was—"Mollie! Mollie Mifflin!" She had to shout for Emily to hear her through the front door, which she refused to open, which was as it should be. "I've read your book! I'm your biggest fan!"

Emily was squinting back through the glass pane in the front door, her face distorted by its bevel. She had no intention of letting anybody come inside her house, rain or no rain, and we can understand her position—an old woman has no business opening her door to a complete stranger, which is what Mollie was to Emily then. Not even to a complete stranger who is a harmless-looking girl. Mollie even told Emily this later after she was settled in and living at the house in the Molenes' employ.

She might have given up and gone away, tried again later maybe. Or she might even have seen the whole thing for the true folly that it was and quit right there—in which case none of what happened would have happened—except that then there was Mr. Molene coming in the gate and up the walk, with Plato panting at his heels. The big black German shepherd was his constant companion. Friendly enough all right, but not the kind of dog you wanted to be fooling around with if he didn't already know you.

So there was Deacon Molene, all gruff and grumpy the way he could get sometimes, and he was wanting to know what Mollie was doing there on his front porch, but it wasn't like he was afraid of her or anything like that—because he had the advantage of the dog, for one thing, and for another, she really was just a bit of a girl without much muscle or meat, and for a third, Deek was not ever afraid of much.

"What's there to be afraid of, at my age?" as he would say himself.

He brushed straight past her into the house, but he left the door open, so she took a chance and followed him right on in.

By all accounts, the place was a mess back then, before Mollie took it over. More of a mess, that is. Two old folks living alone like that, they didn't have the strength to keep it clean, or maybe they just couldn't see it well enough to know how bad it was. Dust balls, layers of grime, fingerprints on the glass and spots on the floor, stains on the carpet, wallpaper faded and torn.

This was all vaguely familiar to Mollie, reminiscent of another old house back in Nowhere—big and dark and ugly—except that one didn't have anybody living in it but ghosts and bums and vermin and bugs. It had long been abandoned by three elderly sisters who lived there and had kept so much to themselves that they were dead for a week before anybody missed them or bothered to go looking for them. Found frozen. Stuck together like a pack of hamburger patties, spooned for warmth in their shared bed. They were comic book crazy ladies, spinsters, hags, and they were pack rats, too. Newspapers piled up to the ceiling. Boxes all over the floor. Books and magazines, milk cartons, old soup cans. And cats all over the place, as well, pissing and pooping and making more cats.

That house became a sort of tourist attraction at first, drawing in the kind of people who will drive around all weekend looking for ghosts and spirits from the other side. Nobody asked the obvious question, which is if it was so cold in there that the three ladies were frozen solid into one clump and it took a truck to get them to the mortuary for a thaw, then how come those cats didn't freeze, too?

Of course, it wasn't nearly that bad for Emily and Deek. They were old, but they were not crazy. They had a maid service that had been coming by once a week to clean up after them, but it is Mollie's opinion that those girls are lazy, and they'll rob you blind, given half a chance. At least that's what her sister Janet always said, and she would know because she used to be one of them herself, before she married the cop and retired into fulltime housewifery, which included taking care of her daughter and cooking for her husband and cleaning a house of her own. Once Mollie was there to help, though, the Molenes had no need for anybody else anymore.

So, sure, they took her in that night. These were kind and generous old souls we're talking about here. Plus, they were still innocent and selfless, then, and on the side of all that's good and holy. Although she did scold them for it eventually, just as the lady in the truck had scolded her, and she did warn them that they should never even think of doing such a thing as that again; still, Mollie was grateful for it at the time. She didn't have a penny to her name—having spent it all on the bus ticket and some magazines to read and food to eat along the way—or anyplace else to go—because their home had been her destination all along. She was on a mission, a quest you might say, and now there she was, completely depleted and at the mercy of fate, without any other options, no plan B.

We know that Mollie came from a family that was good with numbers, especially the kind that add up to something. Her father was an actuary, and he had always told her, among other things: "Cover your ass." Her mother's more domestic and mannerly version of the same advice: "Don't put all your eggs in one basket."

But they were ones to talk, weren't they? Those two, her esteemed progenitors. Mucked up their own lives big time, what business did they have telling Mollie how to manage hers? None whatsoever, not as far as she could see. That big mess they'd made for themselves had definitely trickled right down to her, the younger of their two surviving children, and in fact that's how it was that she happened to be there at the Molenes's door in the first place. She was just hoping for some hospitality, which Deek and Emily gave her in great and generous abundance, no questions asked, and which she constantly reminded herself she had never gotten from her own family and was more than lucky to ever get at all.

They didn't quite know what to do make of her, at first. But once she had explained all about who she was and why she'd come—because she'd read Emily's book, many times, and it had touched her deeply, it had changed her life, so she felt that she just had to meet the author—then Emily invited Mollie to come in, sit down, and have some tea.

She played it cool; she took her time. It wouldn't have done any good to rush them into accepting her as one of their own. That would have to wait. Emily made the tea (weak) and put out some cookies (stale), and they sat in the front parlor (dusty and dim), and it didn't take a genius to figure out that the best way for her to be allowed to stick around for a while (forever!) would be if Mollie could make herself indispensible to them. So, that's what she did. And it wasn't even that hard, because they really were in need of someone like her in their lives just then. She wasn't afraid to work. She would do anything they asked her to do. And then some.

After the tea was cold and the cookies were all gone, Mollie made to be on her way. She said her thank yous and her goodbyes, as polite as you please, and then she slipped around to the back of the house, where Deek had parked their car—a big black Lincoln convertible with comfy red leather seats—and she crawled into the back. Of course, there were plenty of other places she might have holed up that night.

There are kids all over the country who get themselves locked inside a Wal-Mart or a Target store and then find a place there to sleep until morning. And in a college town like Brevity, there were always encampments around, too, home to runaways on the loose, traveling from here to there, following bands or just hanging out on the streets together. There was always someplace to sleep. But Mollie valued her privacy for one thing, and for another, she wanted to stay close. No reason to wander off and make friends or risk a confrontation with a friendly, kindly cop who took a special interest in returning lost children to their bereft parents and forsaken homes.

Instead, she made a pillow of her knapsack and a blanket of the lap rug that Emily kept for use when they went for a drive with the top down, and she curled up to sleep there in the backseat of the car.

She made another attempt at using her clairvoyance by trying to contact her mother that night, but without success. Instead of breaking through the barrier of time and space, just to let Mom know where she was—in case Mrs. Mifflin was worried or wondering or feeling some remorse, which we can suppose was not the case—and that she was in a place that was safe and warm and dry, Mollie bumped right into the Big Nothing. Emptiness. Silence. Not even a flicker.

Not even a peep. Worse than that, she seemed to have invited a violent thunderstorm to gather and strike instead. The kind you read about or see on television after it's over, one that blows through those little farm towns and smashes all the houses flat, tearing up trees and knocking down barns and tossing mobile homes around from one trailer park to the next like a handful of Legos. Where the next day everybody stands around stunned, taken totally by surprise, as if they've been led to believe that somehow because they live in another sort of nowhere that is the middle of America, nothing of any event or consequence is ever supposed to happen to them that might turn their world around and upside down so that everything can never be the same for them again. So stupid-looking that no matter how compassionate you're trying to be you can't help but think that in a way they kind of deserved it?

All that was going on, the blowing and the booming and the flashing and the pouring, but Mollie hardly even noticed, because she was exactly where she wanted to be: safe and sound, cozy as cotton, and sleeping like a baby on the wide warm leather meadow that was the backseat of Emily and Deacon Molene's car.

There was Deek the next morning, up bright and

early—as we have since learned was his daily habit—to take Plato out for his walk and examine the devastation. Soon, too, Emily was out there in her galoshes to try to do what she could to salvage her battered flower garden, which wasn't much. After a while Deek came back and they all—man, woman, and dog—went back inside the house, but Mollie held back. She took the time to run her fingers through her hair, swap one T-shirt for another, put her shoes back on and splash water from a clean puddle on her face, before making her way through the rosebushes around the side and on up to the front door again to knock. No answer, but the house was not locked this time, and that was either a careless oversight or it was a foolishly false sense of safety or it was a timely stroke of luck—either way Mollie took advantage of the situation by simply opening the door and walking in and getting straight to work. As easily as that is how it all began.

The point is this: the arrangement Mollie Mifflin had with the Molenes was not in any way exploitive—neither them of her nor her of them—the way some people might choose (or have been led) to believe. No, it was just a simple arrangement, of mutual benefit to all: she needed them, yes, but they needed her, too. Maybe even more so, if we are to tell the truth. It was that simple. She came along for reasons of her own, and they took her in for reasons of their own, and that's how it came about that she was there, a witness to what happened to them. To what was done. To what they did. And how. And why.

And all right, so what if they were as ancient as a pair of old trees, and feeble and deaf and all that. So what? We might just as well argue that Mollie was only a child, nobody from nowhere, too young and ignorant and innocent to blame. But, she loved them! And they loved her! Didn't she? Didn't they? And isn't that enough?

She was there first thing in the morning and she stayed all day, every day, doing anything that needed doing, until after they had had their dinner (fixed and served by Mollie) and were ready to go up to bed (made and straightened by her), and then she'd leave, go out the front door and creep through the bushes, around the side, to the back, climb into the car again, and sleep. Very quickly they had settled into this routine, and just like that she had become a permanent sort of fixture in their household. Until it seemed they no longer knew what to do or how to get along without her.

Between chores, Mollie explored the house. She considered that to be part of her job as well. She learned about Emily and Deek's habits, witnessed the small sweet demonstrations of their love for each other and the petty humiliations that constantly befell them because of their age and its consequent infirmities. The pills, the aches and pains, the forgetfulness, the minor accidents. Before long she had left the car and moved into the house, and whether they were aware of that or not, what does it matter, really? She worked out a schedule, getting up very early in the morning while they were still asleep. Only Plato heard her creeping around upstairs in the attic on the third floor, above them. He watched her come and go, but he didn't bark or make a sound. In that way he, too, was Mollie's friend. She had him hypnotized, perhaps.

They just accepted her; that's all there was to it, and they insisted on paying her for the work she did for them, of course. It didn't take long, only a few days, really, before it was like she was a part of the family, just as she had dreamed she might someday become. They insisted that she call them Emily and Deek, which she had not presumed to do until then. "No need for formalities," Deek said. With Emily nodding and smiling: "You're our own good girl now, Mollie." Who would want to argue with that?

Some people have already said that Mollie Mifflin was crazy. They've told themselves and each other and everybody else that if her story isn't an outright fib, then it must all of it at least be some weird and complicated wishful dream she had, a delusion, an hallucination, a figment of her imagination that it looks like we're now in the process of turning into a figment of yours.

Or, worse, they think it's just another lie, one among many, this one built to get Mollie out of the trouble she was in at the time. As if she cared about that. A way for her to avoid taking responsibility for the consequences of her choices—some of which, however well-intended, were admittedly ill-advised—or blame for the results of her actions. So she could honestly say that whatever happened, it really wasn't her fault.

Maybe this is true. Maybe Mollie was a liar about this, too. Maybe she was crazy. She was young, but she was not stupid. That much, at least, we know is true.

If we're to have even a whisper of understanding about what happened here, first we'll need to appreciate a few things about the Molenes. To explain why they would do the things they did, we must understand just how much they loved each other. They were married for more than fifty years—that fact will be in the official records of the case—and we can all agree that that's a very long time for two people to be together with one another and no one else, especially now, in our day and age of adultery and polygamy and serial divorce.

Let's just say they were in love, and then we can go on from there to guess that mostly they were happy, too, and yet at the same time, it was their life and it was real, and so it is important to acknowledge, even if only in hindsight, that of course, not all of it was good. There were some days of wine and roses, as Emily would put it, but there also were sure to have been other days of anger and resentment and boredom, heartbreak, even tears, because every couple, especially one that's been together for as long as the Molenes were, has had to survive their fair share of bad times in all of that.

Let's just say there were bound to be some arguments now and then. Maybe even a few full-blown fights. Nothing down and dirty, that's not how they played. Just Emily slamming a door. Or Deek pounding his fist down on the tabletop to make the glasses tip and spill. Emily stomping out of the bedroom, sleeping alone on the davenport downstairs. Deek starting up the car, driving off to who knows where with who knows whom. When she let him know that she didn't understand what it meant to write a check if there wasn't enough money in the bank to cover it. When he got so wrapped up in his work that he forgot he was supposed to meet her for dinner, on her birthday. The time she backed the new station wagon into a light pole; the time he cut the tender branches on the pink magnolia tree back so far that he killed it.

The unexpected success of his first novel, while he was still a young professor with a full load of freshman courses—Prose Comp, Rhetoric, Lit 101. He left the house in the morning and then was gone all day—no word, no phone call, nothing—until after midnight when she saw the skim of his headlights cross the ceiling, heard the car pull into the driveway, and she peered out through the dining room window drapes to see him, drunk and staggering, belting out a garbled version of some old song that he'd heard, unzipping his pants to take a piss on her azaleas. He'd been out ice-skating on the river, barhopping with his students, playing pool with a colleague, driving the back roads to find some legendary fishing hole, gone off all day and into the night, letting himself become absorbed by anything that would keep him out, away from home, avoiding not his wife but his typewriter and that second book, the one his readers were waiting for, the one his publisher had already paid him for, the one that Deek believed was going to either make him or break him, the one he felt compelled to write but could not figure out how to begin.

She'd gone outside in her nightgown and bare feet, wrapped an arm around his waist, supported more of his weight than she would have thought possible as she helped him up onto the porch, through the door, up the stairs and into bed. She brought him ice water and orange juice, dry toast and consommé, nursed his hangovers and didn't complain, just loved him completely, until eventually he was able to muster the courage to face himself and go on with his work.

When Emily's third pregnancy failed and the doctor told her that she and Deek would never have the family they'd dreamed of.

By that time, he had already taken the job at Springer, and they had just moved into the big stick style Victorian on the hill above the campus, and as Emily—home from the hospital and bearing her body as if it were an empty vessel, feeling herself to be as fragile as a bubble of blown glass—as Emily walked through the house its barren rooms had seemed to yawn, as if their gaping silence were mocking her and everything she had until then believed herself to be. She went to bed and sank down into the deep black well of her grief with the covers pulled up, the lights dimmed down, and the drapes drawn shut. If she could have papered over the windows, she would have done that, too. All was shadow. All was death.

As winter thawed into spring, Deek did what he could to wrestle her back out into the daylight of her brighter self again. He stayed home as much as he could and sat through each night refusing to leave her alone, the full length of his body stretched out between a chair and the ottoman he'd pulled up close to the bed that she would not allow him to share with her. He poured tea, warm milk with vanilla, cold ginger ale, brandy, sherry on ice, vodka in a frozen glass. He worked crosswords with her and played hand after hand of gin rummy for a penny a point, letting her win, most of the time. He read to her, too—the fairy tales of her childhood, poetry, even the elaborately sentimental romance novels that she so cherished and he so despised.

By summer he had her sitting up, ready, restless even, to be outside again. He helped her out of bed and brought her downstairs. She sat in the shade of an umbrella while he terraced the back yard with a limestone wall built against its slope, then tore up the grass and turned over the dark dirt. Soon she was up and beside him, on her knees planting the bulbs and roses that still bloomed there twice a year—once in the springtime and then again at the beginning of the fall. Not very long after that she was writing a novel of her own.

The Molenes were married to each other for the better part of their lives—fifty-four years, to be precise. And all that time, Emily said, they were nothing less than the closest of companions. The most passionate of lovers. The truest of friends. They looked into each other's eyes and saw themselves, felt that their understanding of each other might be deeper even than their understanding of themselves. After so much time with Emily, Deek could honestly say he felt as if he had no real being except as his own self could be applied to hers. And she claimed that she couldn't see who she was, either, except in terms of him. It was as if they'd become to one another's separate individual being a reflection, a shadow, an extension of self that neither one of them could or wanted to any more live without.

Chapter Two

If you're thinking that this portrait we've been painting of Emily and Deacon Molene seems just a bit too perfect to be true, then now's the time to toggle in and take a closer look. See them clearly and consider carefully what, by the time that Mollie was to meet them, they had become. There is the massive old Victorian house that they'd called home for sixty years—the plum paint, peeling; the wraparound porch, sagging; the spindled trim, crumbling and cracked. The oldest house in a neighborhood of tree-lined streets and broad front lawns roaring with rider mowers all summer long, it's perched on top of the hill on Market Street at the south end of the Springer College campus, which sprawls across the town of Brevity like the port-wine stain on a young woman's otherwise unblemished face.

Inside, the house is a hush. Its hallways are quiet and dim. The dining room is empty; the kitchen is cold. There's a musty smell of undisturbed dust, old rugs, damp wallpaper, and an overall air of emptiness, neglect, and disuse.

One room that still has some life in it, however, is Deek's study downstairs and to the left of the front hall. Here are shelves that have been filled with a lifetime's unimpeded accumulation of books and exotic knickknacks, the bits and pieces of memorabilia that Emily and Deek have gathered between them over the years. Nothing like Mrs. Mifflin's compulsive collection of ticky-tacky gewgaws picked up at rummage sales and bargain tables all over Nowhere, these include a small brass clock, an ebony goddess, delicately flowered and hinged porcelain boxes, carved wooden bookends, a blown glass ship, and a pair of crystal goblets with naked human stems. The wall behind Deek's big cherrywood desk documents a lifetime lived in the literary limelight—photographs (shaking hands with Aldous Huxley, one arm over the shoulder of Dylan Thomas, tipping a hat to Flannery O'Connor, sandwiched between a young John Irving and a middle-aged Robert Bly), degrees (BA Carleton College; MA Harvard; PhD The University of Iowa), honors (American Academy of Arts and Letters; National Medal of Arts; Associated Writing Programs; Lannan Foundation), and awards (O. Henry, 1953; Aga Khan, 1956; American Book, 1979).

Here, too, is Deek himself, in the flesh: he's sound asleep in his chair. His feet, in brown corduroy slippers, are propped on a padded stool—its needlepoint cushion, stitched by Emily herself many years ago, is frayed at the corners now. A thin book with a worn cloth binding (William Maxwell: *So Long, See You Tomorrow*) lies open on his chest; it rises and falls with his every breath and snore. His hands—liver-spotted and lined, palms calloused, nails horny and ridged—are folded in his lap. The large black German shepherd is stretched out on the rug nearby, and he's snoring, too. The vinyl disk on the old phonograph in the corner skips and repeats, skips and repeats, skips and repeats. Three notes, rising, then falling back to start all over again.

Sunlight shines through the window and casts its beam upon the crags of this old man's face—the sharp wedge of his nose, its cavernous nostrils sprouting coarse dark hairs, his jaw hanging, jowls slack, the overlooked bristles of his beard grizzling his softened chin. His glasses have slipped down. His hair stands up in the wild tufts that Emily finds so endearing, yellowy gray against the shining dome of his mottled scalp. His eyebrows are furry, his forehead is deeply creased—two vertical lines and three horizontal, straight across.

Now, take a look behind Deek, past the heavy drapes and through the mullioned window panes, to see Emily outside in the yard. She's trimming the rosebushes that grow in the curve of the pebbled drive. Gardening gloves protect her small hands from the thorns. She's wearing one of Deek's old plaid shirts, and its sleeves have been rolled back past her bony wrists to expose her papery skin, freckled, bruised, coursed by thin threads of bluish veins. The shirt is buttoned up all the way to her chin; its collar rubs the hanging wattle of her throat. Her black corduroy pants are worn at the knees; she's cinched an orange straw belt tightly around her thickened waist, above the sharper jut of her hipbones. Sloppy white socks sag over the tops of her cracked leather shoes. Her hair has been pulled back, wound up into a loose white bun, glittery with pins. Her round cheeks are flushed, her blue eyes sparkle, her mouth is a pale pink bow.

She's using both hands to wield her clippers; the blades snicker and rose twigs fall to the ground at her feet. Petals are strewn across the grass; drops of pale color are splattered on the browning lawn. Emily drops the clippers, then bends, slowly, painfully, to gather some of the cut stalks. She carries them across the yard and tosses them into a pile near the front gate. She teeters, puts out a hand to stabilize herself.

She does not want to fall. She has to be careful. Last winter the eminent old philosophy professor Ruth Macabee O'Brien lost her footing on the ice outside the library. She slipped, fell, broke her hip, and was dead and in the ground before another two months had passed. Pneumonia, they said it was.

Emily holds onto the fence. She breathes slowly. She feels the warm sunshine on the stoop of her shoulders, waits for the dizziness to pass and her sense of balance to return.

Mollie's view of all this would have been from one of the dormer windows upstairs, in what had become her secret sanctuary on the third floor, in the attic at the front side of the house, facing the street. She didn't have to settle herself in exactly there. Most of the other rooms in the big house had been closed up, and she probably could have taken any one of them with nobody the wiser, but she chose the attic. Because of the window, maybe. And the view. Not to mention the grate in the floor. Once upon a time, the space had functioned as Emily's office, and she did her writing and her reading there, but it was years since she'd been able to climb the stairs to get to it, so possibly she'd forgotten it was ever there. A desk sat beneath the window, and on it, Emily's old typewriter (seafoam green Hermes 3000). No photographs, no prizes, no commendations here. Mollie had wiped away the cobwebs and the dust, and just like that, she'd made the place her own.

The backside of the attic was as full of old junk as the rest of the house, but there it had been piled up every which way—trunks and boxes and odds and ends of furniture that nobody needed anymore. Mollie had cleared out a corner for herself, with a mattress and a table, a lamp and a chair. Plus a small bookshelf and a dresser, a big oval mirror, and a wardrobe for her uniforms, as well as for the dresses, which weren't really hers, of course, they belonged to Emily. Mrs. Deacon Bensenhaver Molene had collected so many pretty things for a woman who'd spent most of her life in the middle of nowhere—there were trunks of ball gowns and cocktail dresses, fancy lingerie, expensive looking suits, hats and gloves and shoes, even her old wedding dress, with its silvery sequined bodice and layered silk skirt belled out by netted petticoats, was boxed up there—and Mollie had had no qualms about scavenging them from their consigned oblivion, pulling them out of the mothballs, and shaking them back to life again for her to wear herself. She was a perfect fit.

Mostly she only put them on when she was alone there, upstairs all by herself, but sometimes if she did

come down dressed in one of those old outfits, Emily seemed to know it. It was clear by her expression: she would be looking at Mollie as if she were also seeing some shadow of herself. That in itself made it worth the risk, as far as Mollie was concerned, that look of recognition in Emily's eyes. And if she stood in front of her mirror and squinted herself into a blur, Mollie could see Emily there in that reflection, too. It was more than just the clothes. Maybe Mollie *was* Emily in some way. Or becoming so. (Because seriously, how can you be completely sure that you are you and not somebody else altogether?)

Deek never seemed to notice, or if he did he didn't say. The practice wasn't hurting anybody, certainly, and there was no way they could have proved it anyway. Plus, Mollie wasn't really in any danger of being caught going through their things, because Deek and Emily were both too old, and she knew they couldn't make it up those steep back stairs to find her there, even if they'd wanted to. Which they didn't, because they trusted her. After all, at that point they had no reason not to.

For Mollie, it was heaven, that attic. Like having a giant flea market all to herself. It was there that she found the goblets. (They were never in Deek's study; we lied about that.)

Both Emily and Deek were a little bit deaf, and although he was the worse of the two, they were both of them in the habit of raising their voices so that the other could pick up what was being said. Which meant that they could not hear Mollie scuttling around above them on her off hours, while when she put her ear to the grate in the floor, their private conversations came in to her loud and clear.

Ironic really, after she'd made it her mission to block out the sounds of her own parents at every opportunity with the old boom box turned up or her headphones firmly implanted in her ears. But that was only because their conversations were always so hideous to hear that nobody would have chosen to listen to them, not even a snoop like Mollie. Accusations and complaints, derision and disapproval, dissembling and blame—nothing at all like the endearments the Molenes shared between them. It didn't matter what the subject was; they were always courteous and polite. They were as respectful of each other as if they'd only just met yesterday, and that wasn't only because they were old and of another, more polite era. Witness your own grandparents, who can hardly ever even talk to each other at all anymore without bickering like birds. Why should they? As far as they're concerned, everything of any interest has already been said and done. That's how time together works, mostly, isn't it?

So now here we have Mollie, she's up in her attic room, she's got her ear to the floor grate, and she's listening to what goes on downstairs. Or she's standing at the window, and she's hidden by the curtain, and she's watching what goes on outside. Deek is snoring in his study. The record is skipping on the player. And Emily is in her garden, balancing herself carefully against the curlicue embellishments of the wrought iron fence that encircles the front yard.

Then, from the front door of a more modern white clapboard house over on Bridge Street near the river, there bursts a young woman in her early thirties. This is Sarah Steele, and in her pink shorts and green T-shirt, she is beautiful to behold. Blond hair, long limbs, slim waist, firm breasts, the works. She crosses the porch, flies down the steps to the sidewalk, and takes off running, up the hill past Mills Avenue, then around the corner toward the boulevards on Grande. Her shoes pound the pavement as her body eases itself into the rhythm of her run. Her heartbeat is strong, her breathing is steady, and her shadow scatters on the pavement as she pursues it through the park and away from the river, around past the performing arts center, the new science building, the chapel, the library, Greek row, the student union.

Emily Molene has left the fence and is tottering toward the sidewalk, carrying another small bundle of her rose clippings to the gutter, where she means to burn them because she has forgotten that curbside burning is no longer allowed; it's been illegal for years. Oh, but when she was young, she'll tell you, on a fall day like this one, the air was always filled with smoke, and the smell of it was delicious.

She is halfway across the sidewalk when Sarah rounds the corner, running toward her, bearing down.

Meanwhile, Mollie has come downstairs to stand on the front porch, and so she sees that Sarah Steele is about to collide with Emily Molene. Or put another way, Emily Molene is about to be bowled over by Sarah Steele. Clearly, the consequences of such an encounter would be bad for them both. So Mollie steps forward quickly; super-hero style, she bounds down the steps, leaps the yard, and grabs hold of Emily's arm. Emily drops the rose clippings and takes a step back as the breeze—rank and pickly, mixed with lemons and something soapy—of the younger woman passes by, her blond hair flying, her fair skin sheened with sweat.

Mollie cries out, curses, and calls her an impolite name (but not the worst you've ever heard) while

Emily gasps and teeters, not sure what's just happened. The back of Sarah's hand is bleeding—a thorn from one of Emily's roses has caught and torn the skin—but she won't notice this until she's home.

Mollie didn't know everything and she couldn't see everything, but here's where she goes off, out of herself and into someone else. It's a sort of clairvoyance, we might say, of the kind that her Aunt Lucy practiced as a psychic and spiritualist in Lilydale, not far from Nowhere, but it's also a trick that she learned that summer, when she was enrolled (at Emily's own urging) in a weekend community writing class with Dr. Peregrine Phillips, professor of English and Director of the Creative Writing Program there at Springer College.

Mollie only went to this class to please Emily and maybe to learn a bit more about reading minds by practicing in public—plus it was free, plus she could pretend to be a Springer student rather than no one from nowhere for a while—so maybe she didn't learn much, but she did learn this: To be a good writer you have to be able to not be you, by which Dr. Phillips meant you're supposed to lose yourself in order to become somebody else. Which turns out to be exactly like mind-reading, in a way.

To do this, he said, you take your own insides and you use them to see and understand another person's insides better. He was talking about when you're making that person up, telling a story about her, but it could be somebody real, too. What's the difference, we might ask, but why provoke an argument.

You gather up all the observable facts—he said "empirical data"—and you put them together to make up the outer image of a whole human being. Black hair, brown eyes, big nose, long ears, tall, short, fat, thin, and so on. Then, you crawl inside to see what you can see. "Understanding breeds empathy, and empathy creates compassion." He wrote that on the board.

So, Mollie didn't know everything, but she knew enough. She knew that if Sarah was anything like her, she was chasing her own shadow as she ran, as if it were proof of her own being, and she would have liked to catch up with it, ask it a few questions, maybe. Like, who do you think you are and what do you want and why are you here? And in her head she would be singing: "I am. I am. I am."

Mollie closes her eyes, and she reads Sarah's mind, and she hears her reciting the Lord's Prayer to herself as she runs. Her lips move with it. "Our Father, who art in heaven…" And so on. Sarah knows it's ridiculous, and she's not sure she even believes in God—at least not that one—but still, she says it because a part of her is just superstitious enough to believe in other worlds and higher powers, so maybe this will somehow work to protect her from harm. The same as when she lies in bed in the middle of the night and names the names and envisions the faces and listens for the voices of those people that she loves the most—whether they seem to love her back or not—as if that will protect them, to keep them safe and sound and sane, and maybe even happy, too.

Other times, Sarah simply counts her blessings. She ticks them off like a shopping list. In her case, it goes like this: "Good health. Nice hair. Long legs. Strong teeth. Handsome husband. Friendly disposition. Promising career." And that's just the beginning. It's a long list. Sarah Steele is a very lucky girl. So far.

Her husband John would tease her if he knew she did this, regularly, and so she doesn't tell him. "What are you thinking about?" he asks sometimes, if he catches her at it. She shrugs, Nothing. Blinks, smiles, as if waking from a dream.

The year before he came to Springer to teach young men and women how to tell the stories that might save their own lives, John Steele published a well-reviewed memoir about how he had survived a nasty childhood with an older brother who was a torturing psychopath, wreaking havoc just short of murder in the lives of his family, his enemies, and his friends before he was bundled off to fight in a war that finally, mercifully, killed him. On the basis of that credential, John was hired to teach creative nonfiction at Springer for a semester with the promise of more time up the road if everything worked out—that is, if the students liked him all right, he wasn't a drunk or a drug addict, and if he kept his hands and other body parts to himself.

As for Sarah, she went where he went, because she was his wife and she was self-employed, so she could do what she wanted to do, wherever she wanted to do it.

Her job? She designed greeting cards. "Heart Strings" was the name of her line. She painted them herself—tepid water colors enhancing hopeful messages, one- or two-liners cribbed from other writers and wiseacres whose work is free for the taking, in the public domain.

Blue sky, billowing clouds, box kite flirting with the sun. Anais Nin: "Throw your dreams into space like a kite, and you don't know what it will bring back. A new life, a new friend, a new love."

A paddle-footed clown shadowed by balloons shaped like bombs. Mark Twain: "The human race has one really effective weapon, and that is laughter."

A pair of wedding bands, entwined against a sunset wash of yellow, orange, and red. Tennyson: "Love is the only gold."

You get the picture.

Sarah was not a real writer like her husband, but she made more money at it than he did, and we might all agree that there is something to be said for that. Her cards were readily available—Target carried them, and Wal-Mart, too. Under the heading: "Sentimental."

In the new house, she did her work in the dining room, which she had taken over as her studio because it had windows on two sides and was full of light. A big table, her paints, her reading chair, and her books. She had her spring consignment to finish that fall—St. Patrick's Day, April Fool's, Easter, Mother's Day, Graduation, Father's Day. And of course there were always birthdays, all year round. And weddings and babies and death.

Dr. Phillips had also been heard to tell his students that if you want to make your characters come alive on the page, you have to give them some memorable physical characteristic, something that says something about who they are so that a reader will be able to identify them right away when they show up again, later in the story. If you can't think of anything for them, then you should borrow something from yourself and use that.

First of all, Mollie raised her hand and asked, "What reader?" That made them all laugh, but she was serious. Dr. Phillips shot back: "Try to imagine that you have readers, darling, and then maybe someday you will" in that sneering tone his voice got when he said something out of the side of his mouth without looking at you when he said it, like squeezing air out of a leak in the bottom of a plastic bag.

Well, all right then Dear Reader of our imagination—whoever you are and wherever you are and when—let's give Sarah Steele a powerful smile, the kind that people respond to, one that she has come to believe in, one that she's learned how to use. Full lips, dazzling white teeth, hint of dimple in the rounded cheek, squint of kindness in the bright blue eyes.

Her mother always told her: "If you want to feel better, all you have to do is smile."

Hence Sarah's inborn optimism. And hasn't it been proven that a smile releases healing hormones into the bloodstream? (So said Aunt Lucy.) Or was it antibodies? We've even heard it said that with laughter you can change the very makeup of your DNA. Even when you don't feel like smiling. Maybe especially when you don't feel like it.

A mother's whispered advice: "Remember it happy, dear." Patting the little girl's knee. Chin set with determination. Eyes furiously dry. "You can't control the world," she said. "You can't control other people. There's just no telling what will happen. No telling what they'll do. But you can control yourself. Get a grip, and then hold on. Hold on with that beautiful God-given smile."

A little girl will take this sort of advice seriously because of all the things she doesn't yet know about the world and about herself. Clairvoyance, for example. Mind-reading and mind-writing, or the fact that this same woman who was at that time her joyfully courageous mother would one day sadden and soften into a languid mass of fear and self-absorption with just enough anger left in her to kick her young daughter out of the house for good.

But that's another story.

For now, here is Sarah Steele, and she's smiling as she runs. What could she be running from? Her past? Not likely, not this girl. She's blessed, remember? Sarah has rounded the corner, she's back on Bridge

Street again, and now she's running toward herself. Toward her life. Into the light of her own future.

"I am. I am. I am," she thinks. And, "Forgive me my trespasses..." And, "Good health, nice hair, long legs, strong teeth, handsome husband, friendly disposition, promising career, gorgeous fall day, lovely new house, quaint little town."

And, "Baby."

Because Sarah Steele knows something that no one else knows, not even her husband, not yet. There is a baby on the way.

In the kitchen of the small white house on Bridge Street, at the edge of the Springer College campus in Brevity, Iowa, John Steele stands at the sink eating his breakfast. Scrambled eggs and hot sauce, straight from the pan. He turns to see his wife come in, sweating and breathless from her run, and he notices that she's bleeding.

He frowns. "What happened to you?"

She examines the back of her hand, wincing, and pulls out the thorn from Emily Molene's rose clipping. He steps aside, and she runs cold water over the wound, feels her stomach roil. She puts her hand on her belly, closes her eyes.

"Are you all right?" he asks.

"Yes. I'm fine."

He squints, cocks his head. "You don't look fine."

She turns to him. Gathers up her smile and dazzles him with it. "I am, though. More than fine. Super."

He nods. All right then. Good. Easier to take her at her word than get her to admit that something's wrong because then she'll have to explain and he'll have to deal with it, and just now he feels he's got problems enough of his own to worry about and withhold.

He has another bite of egg, savoring it. He eyes her calmly—coldly, she thinks—and chews. His eating nauseates her further. The sound of it—sloppy, smacking. The sight—teeth and tongue and macerated egg. The smell. There is a sheen of spattered oil on the surface of the stovetop.

He's offering the pan to her: "Want some?"

She pulls back: "No, thank you."

He shrugs, takes another bite, chews. He disgusts her sometimes, more and more often lately, but she fights the feeling off. She goes to the back door, pulls in a deep breath of fresh air.

"It's such a beautiful day," she says. "We should spend it outside."

When she turns to him again, she sees that he's

frowning. He looks worried. He looks thin. He's been up since dawn, she knows, at his computer, working. The new book must not be going well. She wonders whether she should tell him about the baby now but almost immediately decides against it. Not yet. He isn't ready for it; it wouldn't cheer him up in any way, she knows. Fears. It would only make him feel worse. Instead she says, "Let's make a picnic."

But he shrugs this off, too. Sometimes this unrelenting good cheer of hers irritates him profoundly. "I have too much to do," he says.

She sighs. She should have expected he would say this. Maybe she did expect it. Maybe that's why she suggested the picnic in the first place so that he could reject her and she could feel sorry for herself and be mad at him for that, too. It's Saturday. Does he have to work on Saturday?

Another shrug. Yes, it seems he does. And she needs to finish unpacking and putting away their things.

"Well then, tomorrow maybe?"

But John has dumped the remains of his breakfast in the sink, and now the snarl of the garbage disposal drowns out his reply.

What he said was, "Party."

They will not be able to go on a picnic tomorrow because they'll be at a party, specifically the champagne reception that is being put on to welcome the creative writing students and faculty, old and new, back to Springer for the semester. The engraved invitation is tacked to the refrigerator door by a magnet in the shape of a typewriter, with a handwritten message from Dr. Phillips himself—"Looking forward to seeing you there!"—scrawled carelessly across the bottom in his signature green ink.

We might suppose that John Steele found this attention flattering. Or maybe he was intimidated. Or maybe he thought Peregrine Phillips, PhD, was a pretentious self-absorbed narcissistic overrated ass. He wouldn't have been alone in that, but it's hard to say, and John would not have let on—that job at Springer meant too much to him, and tomorrow it would begin.

Of course his real name was not Peregrine Phillips. We're not going to use his real name here because he's just famous enough that it might be recognized and when he reads this he might find a way to sue somebody for libel or defamation or some such. Although everything we have to say about him is the truth and besides, he said himself that if it's fiction then you're safe from that because you just put a bit at the front about how you made it all up and any resemblance to reality is entirely coincidental, a happy accident of creativity and truth. Call it a novel, he said. Change the names. Change the hair color. Make him tall instead of short or fat instead of thin, a woman rather than a man.

So, all right, here goes.

He's goat-like with deep green eyes and a gap-toothed smile, bearded chin, thinning blond hair, leather bracelet, earrings. He's tall and skinny, and he always wears black, even in the middle of summer when it's hot enough to kill you in a place like Iowa. He grew up somewhere out west, dropped out of school, ran away to New York, lived on the streets, homeless and a dope addict for a while, but all that time he was writing stories, and then he straightened up and went to college and published his books and was hired by a retiring Deacon Molene to run the writing program at Springer, where they love him because he brings in students. His followers are mostly just like him—young men, damaged and disenfranchised, writing about nothing. On purpose.

The other fiction faculty member in the Creative Writing Program at Springer at that time was a woman who called herself Alison Fabricant. We aren't even going to try to hide her identity because that name was already a pseudonym—she had several of them. She thought she was a big deal because when she was young she wrote a novel that got a blurb from John Irving before he stopped giving them, plus a good review from Stanley Elkin before he died. Whoever Stanley Elkin was. Whatever, the book went on from there to win a prize from some organization somewhere, and that was enough to start her thinking that she knew everything there is to know about how to tell a story. She had a reputation for withering criticism and making young women who were only doing their best fall apart, break down, and cry.

"You can't do this," she'd say. "You can't do that." Her voice was shrill, even when she wasn't screaming. "This is crap! This stinks! You have no talent. You should go into business or medicine. Social work. Something useful like that." If you asked us, we'd tell you that whoever it is giving out all those prizes for fiction should be more careful about who they go about recognizing for their work. Give a thought to the poor students who have to suffer the consequences later.

Somebody has a story about a dead horse in the trunk of her convertible, and Professor Fabricant loves it. Or a woman burying the pieces of her father in the garden. Some disgusting bit about a boy's lust for his stepmother. A mother who catches her husband with his nose between his daughter's legs. But if she gets even a whiff of optimism, if she thinks that what you are writing might be uplifting or optimistic, redeeming or romantic in any way, forget it. She won't even read it. Wants nothing to do with it. "It's not real!" she screams. "Life's not like that!" Shrieking like the Red Queen at her most enraged. "Off with your fucking head!"

"But," Mollie murmurs, "of course it's not real. It's a story, that's all."

That's all it ever was. But isn't that enough?

Behind her back, the students called her "Fabricunt."

Two children perched on a throne, legs swinging. The girl in a bright green dress, the boy in periwinkle pants. He leans in to kiss her cheek; she giggles into the bowl of her hands. The poem goes:

If I were a Queen
What would I do?
I'd make you a King
And I'd wait on you.

If I were a King
What would I do?
I'd make you a Queen
And I'd marry you.

Sarah is dappling the scene with sunlight. John is in his office hammering away at the computer keys—whether he's working or writing e-mail or playing solitaire, who knows.

Deek is in his study, reading. Emily is in her bedroom, napping.

As for Mollie, she's in the kitchen, cooking. Vegan meatloaf—lentils, wheat germ, bread crumbs and brown rice. Tofu and broccoli scramble. Baked apples. Quinoa and arugula salad. Fresh bread with soy butter and honey. Everything is healthy, natural and organic, low sodium, low cholesterol, low fat, high fiber, easy to chew and easy to digest.

But not so easy to prepare. It doesn't matter. She has never minded the work, and she doesn't mind the mess, either. This is her job, after all, this is what they pay her for—when they pay her—but she would do it anyway, she'd do it for nothing because it really is nothing but her privilege, and she loves the Molenes more than she ever loved anybody in her own family, including her beloved Aunt Lucy. She would do anything for those two old folks. At this point Mollie Mifflin is truly the happiest girl in the world.

Emily and Deek and Mollie had their dinner together at the big table in the formal dining room, just like a family, mom and dad and daughter—except they were so old and she was so young, she looked more like she might have been their granddaughter. Or great granddaughter, even.

Deek was trying to feed his dinner to the dog, sneaking it under the table bite by bite, but Plato didn't want it either. Emily scolded them both and apologized to Mollie, but that was all right, too. Nothing those two could do would have bothered her.

"It's delicious, dear, really it is." Emily took another small bite. She had the sweetest smile. Her whole face wrapped itself around it like a rose around its bud.

Mollie smoothed the skirt of her uniform over her knees. "I'm so glad you like it," she replied, dazzling back at Emily.

Deek wanted to know what was in the meatloaf, and when Mollie told him, he grimaced and said, "Jesus! No meat?" He pushed back from the table, pulled a cigar out of his shirt pocket, and lit it. Both Emily and Mollie made an admittedly feeble attempt at reminding him again that smoking was a deadly habit—lung cancer, tongue cancer, emphysema, and so on—but he just shrugged. "At my age, my dears, who cares?" And neither of them had a good answer to that, so they let him puff away. The smell got Emily coughing, though, and Mollie craving a cigarette herself, so she fetched him an ashtray, opened a window, and cleared the table. Then, she went outside for a smoke of her own.

If you're thinking that Mollie was insulted or angry or hurt by Deek's ingratitude for all the work she'd done and his rejection of the food she'd made for him, you'd be wrong. She was more generous than that. Completely unfazed, she stood there at the kitchen door and casually smoked her cigarette (American Spirit, yellow), admiring the multicolored splendor of the woods behind the house and ticking off her blessings to herself, one by one. She had a job, she had a home, and she had people who needed her, whether they liked it or not. I am, I am, I am.

Then, a while later, after she had calmed down and finished cleaning up the kitchen—the countertops were swiped, the sink was scoured, and the dishwasher was humming—Mollie came back out into the dining room again, still smiling, to find the Molenes still at the table, just as she had left them.

"Join me?" Deek asked. His eyes were sharp, but

he was offering her a glass of brandy, maybe as a token of apology. She would have liked to think that this was so. At her end of the table, Emily had sagged into a doze, her eyes closed, neck bent, chin on chest. So Mollie figured, why not? Again she took her seat in the middle, between them.

Deek rolled the ash on his cigar, regarded her, then asked her to move close. Again, why not? She scooted her chair toward him, aware of the awkwardness of her feet scrabbling at the floor, the jarring scrape of wood on wood. He smiled, livery lips parting to reveal yellowed teeth, the damp labial wattle beneath his philtrum somehow profoundly obscene.

She was chewing gum, freshening her breath after the cigarette, and then wasn't sure where to put it. Coughed into her fist and held it there in her lap, thought about sticking it under the chair—they would never notice, no one would ever notice. If anything she would be the one to see it and decide to scrape it off. Her fingers pressed, and there was some satisfaction in that. Like carving your name into a tree, sort of. The room was aswirl with cigar smoke. And Emily was no longer only dozing; she was deep in sleep. A little bubble of spit on her lips, sucked in and out. Like a baby. Reminded Mollie of her baby niece, Alicia. She could have watched her forever, but

Janet was always there, dragging her away. Screaming at her—quietly! A fierce whisper—"Leave my baby the fuck alone!" Then kicking her out of the house. Postpartum depression or something like that, Mollie supposed. She wasn't doing anything. She was just watching.

"Do you have a boyfriend?" Deek asked.

She wasn't sure what to say; what did he want to hear? That she did? And that would mean she was normal. Or that she didn't? And that would mean that she was innocent and could be relied upon, completely. All that she knew for sure was that he would not like to hear about Postscript. That was pretty much guaranteed.

She tried to see if maybe she could read his mind, to adjust to what he was thinking—but what he was thinking! She looked at Emily, who was so sound asleep, her hands on the table, the lace placemat. Her dress—what she wouldn't know is that she'd dribbled on herself. Her face slack. The brown spots on the backs of her hands. How easily she bruised, and her skin was like tissue paper, easily torn.

Old age, this is what it looks like. Mollie's dad had been fond of saying: "We're nothing but walking corpses. Headed for a certain death. Worms. In one end and out the other."

Mollie sniffed. A smell of urine. And roses.

Deek was regarding her. "Drink up, dear," he said. "This is a treat!"

Mollie took a sip. She could feel it in her nose. She coughed, then coughed again.

Deek smiled, delighted. "You're just a child, aren't you?"

She might have argued this, but he went on: "How glad I am for your company, my dear. Nice to have someone young in the house. To bring some life to us here. Imagine what it was like for me, as a young man, coming here, to this college, all the young women. You can guess. I was in heaven. Or was it hell? Married, after all, wasn't I."

Picking tobacco off his lip. The cigar in the ashtray, wet from where he'd sucked on it. Poured another splash of brandy for himself. Offered the bottle to Mollie: "Another one?"

His hand was on her knee, but he didn't mean anything by that, did he? He was a very old man. Maybe he didn't even know that it was there. She wasn't sure whether she should try to pull away or stay put. Would he be offended? She concentrated. Looked at Emily. *Wake up. Wake up!*

And just like that, at the end of the table, she did. Emily came to, flailing like a baby startled out of a nap. Deek pulled his hand away and twinkled at Mollie. He threw back the rest of his brandy as she stumbled to her feet, feeling guilty, as if she'd been caught at something, but what?

"Will you be needing anything more from me tonight then, sir?" she asked, standing up and doing her best proper English maid impression with a little curtsey thrown in for added authenticity.

"No dear, you can be on your way now," Emily said, ever the privileged lady. "Go off and have some fun, why don't you? We'll manage things from here now, won't we Deek?"

He nodded. "Indeed we will, my darling," he said. "Everything's copasetic. I've got it all under control."

So Mollie said good night, as usual, and headed for the kitchen. Then, she made a big business of turning off the lights and slamming the door before creeping up the back stairs to the attic, where she'd be putting her ear to the grate again, as usual. She wanted to hear what they said to each other, which as it turned out, wasn't much.

Deek helps Emily on the stairs; they're on their way up to bed. Plato follows, patiently. Deek's hand is on the banister; hers is on his arm.

"Okay," he says, "here we are. Steady as she goes."

"I am not a boat, Deek." Emily frowns, purses her lips, and her face collapses in upon itself. She stumbles, and he catches her. Her weight against his body is like air; she's his bird with hollow bones.

"Whoa there," he says, his voice low and soft. "Slow it down a bit now. Nice and easy. Upsy-diddle. Here we go."

She has stopped.

"What?" he asks, fearing that maybe he's hurt her feelings now, with his baby talk.

She wavers, then steadies herself again. "I think I'm getting too old for this," she says. Her voice is so soft, so faint, that Mollie can barely hear her.

"For what?" he asks.

She looks around at the house, the entryway below them, the hall, the doors to the rooms beyond. "For this." Her arms sweeps in a wide gesture of inclusion. "All of it. The great grand spectacle of life."

Deek sighs. He releases her arm. He sits down on the stairs, and she drops next to him. "Maybe we should think about moving our bedroom downstairs?"

He looks at her with genuine fondness, deep love. His hand—shaky, palsied, skin dappled with age spots, and one fingertip missing from when he dropped a cinderblock on it—touches her small head.

Her hair, which used to be thick and dark, is now a wisp of smoke. "There ought to be a way that we could trade ourselves in," he says. "Like a couple of clunkers."

She shakes her head at him. "But I'd miss it. The old you, I mean."

"You'd get used to it, I think."

She takes his hand, holds it in her own. "If I could wish for anything, Deek, do you know what it would be?"

"What's that?"

"To be young again."

"I'm too tired to be young."

"If you were young, you wouldn't be so tired."

The dog sits down on the steps next to them. He whimpers. Puts his chin on Deek's knee. Deek has wrapped an arm around his wife. She rests her head on his shoulder.

"Lucky Mollie," she says. "She's so young. She still has her whole life ahead of her."

Mollie nods. Yes indeedy, she's thinking. Lucky little old me.

By this time Mollie had been in Brevity, living with and caring for the Molenes, for three months, and she had established a regular routine, both for herself and for them, waking and dressing in the pre-dawn hours, when they were still asleep, using the second floor bathroom at the far end of the hall, where they would not see or hear her, even if they were to awaken and be up and about for some reason, which was never very likely. What had been a maid's bathroom was at the top of the back stairs that led down to the kitchen.

Only once or twice was there a close call for Mollie to contend with in this arrangement, when Emily complained about noises in the attic and Deek supposed there must be squirrels up there. Vermin? But no, not vermin, only Mollie Mifflin. He called an exterminator to come by in an act of independence and self-reliance that actually took Mollie by surprise—when the man showed up at the front door and insisted she show him the way to the attic—as Deek and Emily both had settled nicely into a habit of depending almost entirely upon Mollie for most things by then.

She could easily have hidden her own traces if she'd been forewarned of the inspection and given a little time to do it, but as it was, all she could do was stick to the guy, follow him up the attic stairs with her heart in her throat. He poked around up there, but she made like the light switch was broken, and he did not question this, just whipped out his flashlight as if it were his most treasured appendage. At least he was limited by the circle of its beam, which was focused not on the contents of the attic, but on its floor, the corners, cracks, and crevices that would reveal to him what he needed to know. Which was nothing, basically. If there was a rat in there, he was it himself. Nasty man. He put out poison, and that was the extent of it, except Mollie saw him stop before the mirror and consider his reflection in it, her own ghostly self hovering behind him. He caught her eye and held it a moment too long, which was suggestive in a way that she let him know she knew and felt, there in the dark. He let the flashlight beam fall and in the darkness turned to her. Hand on her breast, then. A squeeze, that was all. She let him have that, why not? The warmth of his breath in her hair. And then she pulled away and let him follow her down the attic stairs as she promised that yes, she'd replace the bulb up there ASAP, and he promised that the poison would drive any vermin crazy with thirst, out of the house to find water, so there would be no rotting corpses in the walls.

After he was gone, Mollie had to exterminate the leavings of his presence there herself. The smell of his aftershave, the same as her father wore. His footprints in the dust. The poison itself. Blinded by his own intentions, he had found nothing else, and so Mollie's presence there went undetected. "Don't worry," she told Emily and Deek. "It's all been taken care of." If they complained again, she told them it was just the wind. Or some such as that.

Mollie had made the mistake of giving her sister the Molenes' address, and right away her mother was sending letters, wanting to know when she was planning to come back home to Nowhere again. As if she were a runaway or something. As if it hadn't been Mrs. Mifflin's own idea to kick her daughter out of her life in the first place.

There was Emily standing on the front porch with a postcard in her hand, "This one seems to be for you, dear." Mollie apologizing, embarrassed by her own audacity, taking advantage of Emily's generosity, acting as if she had a place there with them, as if the Molenes' home were her own. "You should write your mother back," Emily said. "I think she misses you."

Dear Mollie, When will I see you again?

Dear Mom, Never!

She knew full well her mother didn't miss her. It was just that once she found out that Mollie was settled in and on her own, financially independent and emotionally stable, once it looked like she was maybe going to be okay after all and no thanks to anybody but herself, well that's when Mom just couldn't stop herself; she had to butt in. And once Dad was out of her hair, too, same thing. Once she'd finally gotten what she'd always wanted, which was: that whole crappy house to herself, without Mollie around causing trouble and making little messes for her to have to clean up. Without her husband coming up behind her to pinch her ass or give her a peck on the back of her neck. She had two reactions to this behavior—she would squeal and slap at him or mutely brush him off until he quit. But, as it often happens, once she'd finally got them both out of the way, that's when she started wanting them both to come back. If not him, then at least her. Too late, Mollie said. He was gone for good, and so was she.

And if that hurt Mom's feelings, Mollie honestly didn't care, plus she didn't believe it anyway. All that sob, sob, poor me—old story, we'd heard it already, plenty of times before. Mrs. Mifflin was always feeling sorry for herself about something, going on about how hard her life was, how put upon she was by everything and everyone—the world, the weather, her job, her boss, the patients, her husband, her children. It was everybody all just one big pain in her ass.

And then she had the nerve to ask, when was Mollie coming home?

One more time, with enthusiasm: "Never!"

Except lately Mollie has been thinking that maybe she could go back some day, now that she's sort of famous. She could bring along a news team, maybe, like that guy who wrote that book and then went home again with Oprah's camera crew tagging along behind him, documenting it all. He even published a story about it, twice, once in a magazine, and then again in a book of essays about himself. That's the way to do it, Mollie says, celebrity-style, entourage and all. Go home and thumb your nose at all those high school shitheads who made your Nowhere life miserable, driving you to the drugs and drink that were supposed to eventually kill you.

It's the resentment that does it. Letting that stuff get to you, allowing it to eat away at your soul. You have to get that out of your system first, and then you can go home to Mom and write an essay about it so that she has to say she's sorry. And then you can forgive her. In public, cameras rolling, reporters taking notes.

Deek and Emily have been doing this for years, and always it's the same. He is in the bathroom, looking at himself in the mirror. He used to have to shave twice a day, but now he hardly has any hair left on his body at all. Bandy legs. Narrow hips. Big belly. Sunken chest. He turns away.

Emily is at her dressing table, contemplating her own reflection. The fallen skin on her face. The weakening of her chin. The thinning of her hair. She takes the pins out and lets it fall down her back.

Deek has come out of the bathroom, and he's standing in the doorway, watching her now. Emily turns and can see his outline, the question mark of a stooped old man in baggy pajamas. He sees her, in turn, diminished and so small, as if a lifetime has sucked itself out of her being, which basically it has.

He brushes her hair, gently, tenderly, and braids it for her. And then they climb, creaking, into their bed. She rolls up close to him, and he reaches out, gathers her in. They hug and snuggle like that for a bit. You wonder, do they have sex anymore? Not likely.

Does it matter?

Meanwhile, over on Bridge Street, John Steele moves through his house, checking locks and turning off lights. Sarah is already asleep. He sits on the edge of the bed to take off his shoes. The reading lamp is on. She's on her back, a book lies open on her chest.

When he picks it up, she stirs and rolls over onto her side, away from him.

He takes a look at the book. It's a battered paperback, its spine broken, its pages yellowed with age. *Forevermore* by Emily Molene. The faded watercolor on the cover depicts a pair of goblets, their glass a frosted swirl of smoky blue, their bowls fluted, each supported by a stem that forms the perfectly rendered body of a woman on one and a man on the other. Heads thrown back, hair flowing, arms upraised, hips turns just enough to cast the private parts discreetly into shadow.

John sets the book aside, undresses, and climbs into bed. Tugs at the covers. Puts a pillow over his head. This is how John and Sarah Steele sleep, not spooned but back-to-back.

And then it was the middle of the night in Brevity, Iowa, but Mollie was still awake. She was bug snug on her cot up in her attic room, reading by the lamplight, and she was thinking to herself: This is the life, isn't it? Doesn't get any better than this. And it wasn't just anybody's life. It was hers.

Downstairs, just below her, Mollie's benefactors slept. On the floor beside their bed, Plato was dreaming, his nose twitching and paws moving as he chased the rabbits of his puppyhood. Looking back, we might suppose that if Mollie could have seen Emily and Deek just then, maybe she'd have had a forewarning of exactly how limited her time there with them really was. Moonlight spilling in through a crack in the drapes and shining on their faces, making them look withered and craggy, shriveled and ugly and old.

But Mollie was innocent, and to her, the situation was still perfect because it was all that she'd ever wanted for herself. A place to live. A job to do. A couple of good people to love and love her back. She was wishing for nothing else then but that what was would never end. It would never change. It would stay just like that, on and on, forevermore.

FOREVERMORE

by
Emily Molene

Paris, 1949. Leo and Alice Bell had been married for three days, and they were at the end of their honeymoon, the whole of which had mostly been spoiled by rain. They'd spent that afternoon in the Louvre, again, and were on their way back to their hotel, both of them downcast and doing their best not to quarrel, but now after an hour of wandering, they both had to admit that they were lost. Whose fault was that? It was difficult to tell. Neither wanted to blame the other although Alice was able to speak French and Leo had the map and so it must have been that one of them had done something wrong. Thunder grumbled in the distance, and the narrow cobbled street was wet and dark, an obstacle course of fetid puddles and scattered piles of garbage and debris. Leo was trying to hurry his young wife on toward what he thought was a main thoroughfare ahead, but she held back, stepping carefully, worried for her shoes, which were new and had cost her more than she had meant to pay. He guided her around a corner and abruptly stopped. Three dogs were tearing at a large, unidentifiable piece of meat that could as easily have been the body of a small child as some unlucky family's Sunday roast. Two of the dogs were mongrels and too absorbed in their meal to notice Leo and Alice, but one, a large black German shepherd, raised his head.

His eyes were yellow, and wary. His growl was deep-throated, and low. He bared his teeth, threateningly. Blood shone on his muzzle.

Leo and Alice backed away, slowly. The mongrels looked up from their meal, and all three dogs watched the couple as they edged around the corner.

"Now!" Leo shouted, grabbing her arm.

They turned abruptly and began to run, never mind the new shoes.

The mongrels went back to their grisly meal, but the black shepherd's ears were perked and his muzzle was raised, as he sniffed the air, pensively. Suddenly he began to bark as he tore off in pursuit of the fleeing pair.

"This way!" Alice screamed, wobbling on her heels, turning down another cobbled street.

A warm yellow light spilled out onto the sidewalk from the window of a shop in the middle of the block. Alice ran for it, with Leo close behind her. The black dog rounded the corner, and the bell above the door chimed as Alice stumbled in, followed by Leo, who slammed the door behind him with bang.

Alice looked around. They were in a crowded shop, full of an odd collection of curios, statues, framed watercolors, old books, antique odds and ends. Leo was at the window. He wiped a circle of grime away from the glass with his fingertips and peered through to see the black dog standing in the yellow spot of a streetlight, gazing back at him. The dog sniffed the air again, then turned and slowly loped away.

Alice was exploring the shop, marveling at its odd collection of statues and dishes and urns, bottles and books and toys. Leo turned to follow but soon stopped, his attention drawn to a large glass jar. Inside, some strange fleshy thing was floating. He reached out to touch the side of the jar, and as his fingertips skimmed the thick glass, Alice squealed. He yanked his hand back and looked up.

"Alice?"

He made his way through the clutter to the back of the shop. He rounded a blind corner and found himself face-to-face with a tall thin woman who was dressed all in black. Her arms and hands were ornamented with an assortment of bracelets and rings. Her eyes were the milky blue of the blind. Alice was standing next to her, looking startled.

"Goodness," Alice said. "You scared me half to death."

The blind woman apologized, and Leo told her how they'd been chased here by a dangerous-looking black dog.

Alice's attention had been drawn to a particular glass shelf. "Oh, Leo," she said. "Look at that."

He saw that she was pointing to a pair of goblets. She reached for one, but just as her fingers were about to close around the stem, the blind woman's hand snapped out and clasped her wrist. "Careful!" she exclaimed.

Alice quickly pulled her hand away.

"You don't want that," the blind woman said.

"I don't? Why not?" Alice was a person who always wanted most whatever she was not supposed to have.

"Too dangerous."

"But it's really lovely. I don't think I've ever seen anything so..." Unable to resist, she was reaching out again, and this time she picked the goblet up. She turned it in the light. It was exquisite, the glass a frosty swirl of color, the stem the perfect rendering of a naked man. "He looks so real!" she exclaimed.

The blind woman nodded. "So I've heard," she said.

"How much is it?" Alice asked.

Leo tried to interrupt, but the blind woman replied, "Too much."

Alice persisted. "How much is too much?"

"Two thousand francs."

Alice smiled. "I can give you fifteen hundred."

Again Leo tried to stop her. "Alice, what are you doing?"

She was reaching for the small silk bag that she'd pinned inside the bodice of her dress.

"Seventeen-fifty," the blind woman said.

"Seventeen-fifty?!" Leo exclaimed. "That's almost... what? Three hundred dollars. Alice, we can't afford..."

But Alice wasn't listening. "Each?"

The blind woman grinned. "Both!"

Alice had pulled out a handful of crumpled currency. She counted it out for the blind woman, whose grasp was quick as she snapped up the bills and they were gone. Leo threw up his hands as the blind woman wrapped the goblets in newspaper.

She told them how to find the main boulevard, which wasn't far, and when they stepped outside the shop it was still raining, but at least there was no more sign of the black dog. Leo held the umbrella, and Alice carried the package, and they were able to find their way back to their hotel without any trouble.

When they were in their room, she gently set the package down on a table. "And you told me I don't know how to dicker," she said, smiling at her husband.

He picked up the package and started to open it.

"Careful," she warned.

"Careful? Alice, these cost us a fortune. I'll treat them as if they were gold!"

"It was not a fortune."

"But it was an extravagance. Alice, we're not rich. You have to remember that now."

"Rich in love maybe." She began to unbutton her sopping dress, as Leo moved to the desk at one end of the room. On it sat an old typewriter with a piece of paper rolled into it and some manuscript pages piled nearby, along with a scatter of reference books and magazines. The manuscript title page read, "The Lost Cause, a novel by Leo Bell." Leo tapped this with his fingertips, then bent to look at the paper in the typewriter. He leaned forward and rolled it out, read it, rolled it back.

"Love," he said, distracted. "Yes, of course, love."

"You don't like my goblets?"

He smiled. "I like them very much."

She had stepped out of her dress and now stood before him in her lacy slip. Behind him, the window was filled with dismal rain. As he turned to look out at it, his smile faded. "But you have to remember, Alice," he said, "that tomorrow our honeymoon will be over. And after that… real life."

She came up behind him, put her arms around his waist, leaned her cheek against his back. "Sounds like fun."

"We're likely to have some bad times, Alice."

"Better or worse, remember?"

"Nothing's ever what you hope it will be."

"Mm-hmm. But someday you're going to be a famous author, Leo. And we'll live in a big old house that I'll fix up. We'll have lots of children. And lots of friends. We'll travel wherever we want to go, and we'll see everything there is to see, and we'll have everything we've ever wished for, and we'll be the happiest people that anybody ever met."

"Happily ever after. Is that it?"

He turned to look at her, still troubled. She studied his face for a moment.

"Leo, it's our honeymoon," she said, her mouth in a kittenish moue. "Here we are in Paris, we have our whole future ahead of us, whatever it holds in store. I think we should be celebrating. Let's don't mope now, please?"

She opened the package with the goblets in it.

"I'm not moping," he said.

Alice handed the female goblet to him and kept the male one for herself. She picked up the bottle of brandy that was sitting on the desk next to his typewriter. "Yes, you are too."

He studied the goblet's stem and ran his thumb over the generous curve of its body. "Maybe just a little," he admitted. When he realized what he was doing, embarrassed, he stopped.

Alice was smiling. "Maybe that's what that old witch meant when she said they were 'dangerous.'"

She filled Leo's goblet with brandy, then her own. She raised hers in a toast and waited until he lifted his.

"Here's to us then, Leo," she said.

"To Mr. and Mrs. Leo Bell."

She touched her glass to his. "To our happiness."

"To our life together."

Outside, it had begun to rain hard again. There was lightning in the distance. A soft roll of thunder far away.

"To your fame."

"To your beauty."

The rain came harder. The lightning flashed closer, the thunder was loud.

"To our love."

Leo was smiling. Alice was gazing into his eyes. They each took a sip of the brandy. Then he set his goblet down and reached for her, and in the heat of their embracc her mouth found his...

CHAPTER THREE

The party was really just a cocktail reception at Dr. Phillips' house. It was a little shindig he threw every year to welcome the new students and faculty to the creative writing program. Every year Emily and Deek were invited, and every year they went. Mollie had not been explicitly included in the invitation, but she figured it was a part of her job to look after the old couple, even though it was a Sunday and officially her day off, so she might as well go, too. Emily didn't insist, of course, but Mollie could tell she wanted her to be there. Anyway, she was curious, and she didn't mind a party—free food, harmless small talk, and a good place to practice her ESP. Besides, sometimes it was lonely for her all by herself up in the attic. Every now and then, a girl needs to get out. Mollie had no friends and no social life to speak of, no life at all, in fact, beyond her connection to the Molenes. She missed Postscript sorely, but also her family, believe it or not, in a stupid, sappy way that we might understand was actually more nostalgia for her old self, back when she was a kid and didn't know any better than to care about the people that she was related to by blood whether they cared the same for her in return, or not.

There was only so much looking-after that the Molenes would allow, however, and so Deek did the driving, with Emily in the front seat with him and Mollie in the back of the Lincoln like a little kid on an outing with her parents. Make that grandparents. Or great grandparents. Sitting with her seatbelt fastened and holding on with both hands, queasy from the herky-jerky way he crept the car along the streets, while Emily pointed out the obstacles as if he couldn't see them for himself, which probably he couldn't. Who is it that would issue a driver's license to a tremorish, half-deaf old man with eyes scummed by cataracts and the reaction time of a sloth?

Plus, Mollie suffered from what might well be described as an inborn tendency to brace herself for the worst that might happen, just in case it did. She had learned that kind of thinking from her father. "Keep your hopes low," he liked to say, "and then you'll never be disappointed by your life." Or, "Don't aim any higher than you can reasonably reach." He was an actuary, as we've said, a statistician that the insurance companies hire to crunch the numbers that will tell them the mathematical likelihood of a certain outcome. Such as: injury or death, disease, fire, flood, catastrophe, all kinds of bad timing and bad luck. 48% of all automobile accidents are fatal. A passenger in the back seat of a car as a 17-37% chance of survival in a head-on collision, depending on whether it's with another car moving at the same speed, a concrete barrier, or a tree. 82% of all car crashes occur within three miles of home. Shattered glass, twisted chrome, broken bones, internal injuries, head trauma, severed limbs—everything will have its odds.

The party had been announced as an open house, and the Molenes were never in any hurry to do anything, so they weren't the first to arrive, which meant that the street was already packed with cars, and all the handicap spots had been taken. Deek parked at the curb as close as he could get, which was about a half a block off, and he used his cane to help him wobble along in a way that favored his left hip, while Mollie had Emily by the elbow to help her find her footing on the cracked sidewalk. That was when she noticed that the old woman was wearing two different pairs of shoes—a black velvet slipper on one foot and a pink leather flat on the other—but there wasn't anything to be done about it then. You can argue if you want to that

Mollie should have seen it sooner (and don't think she didn't beat herself up plenty about that later) because if she had it's very possible that things would never have gone to where they went that night. But the fact is, Mollie didn't notice it until just then, and there's nothing in the world that we can do about that now.

Peregrine Phillips' house was a landmark in Brevity, so different was it from the older buildings that made up the campus of Springer College. In fact, some people complained that it was a modern monstrosity, all curves and odd angles, made out of concrete and steel and glass. And standing there in the fancy marble foyer: Dr. Phillips himself. Deek introduced Mollie, referring to her as "our girl," which she found flattering. It seemed as good a definition of her as any. She was just a girl, after all, and at that time still more than happy to be theirs.

Mollie was not much for being one in a gathering of strangers, so she lurked at the edges, eventually taking a seat against the wall in an out-of-the-way spot where she would be able to see without being seen. There was Deek, leaning on his cane—a living caricature of the old academic that he was, in his worn tweed jacket, baggy pants, white shirt, bolo tie. And there was Emily, too, tottering amiably through the crowd with a quizzical little smile on her face, as if she wasn't sure where she was or who all those people were. She was balancing a glass of champagne in one hand and a piece of skewered chicken in the other, and as she turned away to take her place beside her husband, Mollie noticed that the hem of her sweeping flowered dress was lopsided, because she had it buttoned up all wrong in the back. Something else Mollie should have seen sooner, you might say. But again, there it is: she didn't.

It's John Steele who approaches Dr. Molene—he comes forward and shakes the older man's hand, introduces himself, has to say his name three times before Deek understands it, but still, whether he knows who John is, that isn't clear. He leans toward him with a pained look on his face as he strains to hear above the deafening drone of raised voices echoing off the windows and the walls in the minimalist front room of Dr. Phillips' modern house.

Regarded from a distance, John looks very much like a younger version of Deek. The resemblance between them is remarkable enough to make Mollie wonder, Does no one else see this? It isn't in the details—one man is tall and thin (John) and the other is short and thick (Deek)—but in the overall sense of them, and standing face-to-face as they are, it's as if *he* might have been the mirror reflection of *him*, and vice versa. A funhouse mirror that playfully distorts an observer's perception maybe, but again it isn't about the details. They stand the same way—Deek has his left hand on his cane and John has his right hand on the back of a chair—and each leans toward the other at an angle that gives the sight of them together a pleasant symmetry of composition.

You could have begun to imagine what John was going to look like as an old man. And what Deek had been when he was young. Stoop the one and straighten the other. Add wrinkles here, remove hair there. Take away the glasses, or add them, either way.

You might have been tempted, too, to listen in, to hear what those two had to say to one another, and you might suppose that Deek is suspicious of this memoir writer who can't help but be making his story up in some way, for blame or for redemption or for something else in between. While John will be amused by the old man, whom he must know to be no real threat to him in the long run. What are they talking about? Not their books, each other's or his own, because neither has read the other and both want to hide that fact. So, what? The weather? All the rain over the summer, the storms, what John has to look forward to in the winter yet to come. Anybody listening in might expect more than this from these two men of letters, but that expectation will be sorely disappointed. They have nothing to say to each other, it seems, and their parting is awkward as Deek begins to search the crowd for his wife, and John drifts dreamily away, back again toward the bar.

Somebody says, "Mushroom?"

Mollie looks up, and there he is. This will be her first sight of Doyle Hirleman: curly blond hair, sky blue eyes, melt-your-heart smile. He is standing in a spotlight of late afternoon sunshine that comes streaming in through the window and hits him just so. Later, when they step outside for a smoke, he'll tell her his name and explain that he's not a teacher or a writer, either. He's just another working stiff like her. He's in uniform, too—white shirt, black pants, red tie—and he's holding out a tray of stuffed mushrooms in one hand, a stack of cocktail napkins in the other.

She takes one of each. Chews demurely. Dabs at her lips. He's eyeing her, or maybe he's just peering into the shadows between the buttons of her uniform blouse. There's that smile again, before he turns away to thread through the crowd toward the kitchen, and then, like a vision, he is gone.

We have a photo from this party. It's of John and Sarah Steele flanking Emily and Deek Molene—Emily in her mismatched shoes; Deek leaning on his cane. Sarah aglow in the first fair blush of her pregnancy, and John in a cavalier pose, one fist at his hip and a peanut can in his other hand, raised as if in a toast. There is Mollie, too, hovering in the background, an angelic glimpse of white smudge in a corner of the frame.

Plus, she has kept a few mental snapshots of her own:

Deek, introducing himself to Sarah, gallantly kissing her hand. Or was it pervily?

John Steele at the bar, ordering another scotch and soda, fiddling with the peanut can, looking over his shoulder, keeping an eye out for his wife.

Dr. Phillips bleating at the shapely slut in the scanty green fringed dress, who basks in the glow of his attention and casts looks around to see whether anyone else has noticed, locks eyes with Mollie, shares what looks like a conspiratorial smile.

Emily perched on a chair in the living room, studying her shoes.

A pair of middle-aged faculty wives at the food table, gossiping about the history professor who ran off with a student last year. Their husbands in the kitchen discussing blood pressure levels and cholesterol counts.

Mollie and Doyle outside on the screened back porch, sharing a smoke and getting to know each other, starting with the vitals—name and occupation—before moving on to bigger things like, Where are you from? How did you end up here? And, What are you doing later tonight?

He's a townie, born and raised in Brevity. He wants to make films someday. He cares about animals. Volunteers his time at a homeless shelter. Definite hero material, he is out to save the world, just like Mollie. He invites her to join him later at the Grotto, a bar down on Main Street, and she is thinking maybe she'll go or maybe not, but ultimately she does, and he is there, and together they…

But we're getting ahead of ourselves. First, there was the drive home, and Emily's despair when she told Deek about the shoes, and Deek's grim suggestion after he'd rebuttoned her dress in the back. And then after that, before the night was over, there would be the thunderstorm and the music, the goblets and, of course, the wish.

A few more things worth mentioning also happened before Mollie and the Molenes left the party that evening. First, John and Sarah Steele had a spat, then Emily got her feelings hurt, and finally Mollie lost her temper.

It started at the bar. Apparently Sarah had already said something to John about his drinking, and that explained the part about the peanut can. He was using it to hide his glass of Scotch. Everybody but Sarah thought this was pretty funny when it was discovered. Their laughter brought tears to her eyes, but she managed to be a good sport about it nevertheless. Dr. Phillips put an arm around her shoulder and told her not to worry. "We're like a family here," he said. "We'll take good care of John."

A bunch of writers and academics, an open bar, what else would you expect? These eggheads can drink and talk forever; they think they know everything, and given half a chance they'll tell you all about it, too bad for the more modest little wife who is pregnant and so prefers to stay sober. To her credit, though, Sarah didn't get mad, and she didn't cause a scene. She bit her tongue and flashed that smile, then made a break for the ladies' room down the hall.

The bathroom was occupied, and the three other women who were standing in the hallway waiting for their turn welcomed Sarah into their midst. Among them was none other than Fabricunt herself, whose voice carried like a whole pawful of claws on slate. She made a big deal about greeting Sarah, all smiles and gracious introductions, and then after that was over with, the scene went something like this:

One woman, a slightly overweight, immaculately groomed Texas Republican type with gold earrings and sparkly pink lipstick says, "Golly, did you see Emily Molene?"

Fabricunt nods, sadly shakes her head. "Such a shame."

"Did you see her dress?" asks the other woman. This one is petite and curly and as annoyingly eager as an overbred toy poodle.

"And those shoes," says the Republican.

Fabricunt adds, "He seems to be failing a bit now, too, doesn't he?"

"It's cute how they still seem to love each other, though," says the Poodle. "Like a couple of kids."

Fabricunt considers this. "Maybe," she says, "but if you stop to think about it, they can't have much longer, can they? To live, I mean."

Now Sarah pipes up; she can't help herself, that's how sweet and good she is. "What an awful thing to say."

Fabricunt does not like being criticized, and she

bristles. "I'm sorry. I know it's not easy. But it's only the truth. Face it, or be damned."

The Poodle jumps in, nodding vehemently. "She's right. For example, that house they're in. Why, I'll bet Emily can't even get up the stairs anymore without his help."

"They have that girl, though," Fabricunt puts in. "She's a nurse, isn't she?"

The Republican smirks. "She's a kid. She'll quit."

The Poodle frowns. "I've heard Emily say they're going to have to carry her away from there before she'll ever leave."

Fabricunt revs up. "Well," she says, "I personally think that's irresponsible. I mean, just look at the two of them. What are they, almost ninety years old now? Emily can hardly take two steps without toppling over. And Deek. Every time he gets behind the wheel of that car it's a miracle nobody's killed. Have you seen him drive?"

The Poodle whimpers, "But as long as they have each other…?"

The Republican nods. "I suppose one of them will have to die first…"

And then Fabricunt opines, as if she knows what she's talking about, "Once one goes, the other won't be far behind." They all take a moment to ponder this as she lights a cigarette, shakes out the match, and blows a thoughtful cloud of smoke.

"My guess is it will be him first," says the Republican at last. And then she adds, "I just hope I die before I ever get to be that old. When I start looking like that, somebody shoot me, please?" Her fingertips fluff her hair.

Just then the bathroom door opens, and out steps Emily Molene. You can just tell that she's heard everything. The women have been stunned into silence, but Emily only smiles. "I do beg your pardon, ladies. Are you squeamish about death?" Fabricunt blinks, and Emily goes on, "Well then, just how do you think my husband and I feel, knowing how close we are to it? Imagine, if you will, waking up in the morning all aches and pains, feeling your own body deteriorate right out from under you." She nods at Fabricunt's cigarette. "Better to die young, I'd say, wouldn't you, dear? Kill yourself quickly? Get out while the getting's still good?"

Frowning, Fabricunt smashes her cigarette out in an ashtray on the hall table, the other two women gape, and Sarah slips into the bathroom, as Emily gathers up her dignity and totters off to find Deek.

He was engaged in a conversation with a spidery-looking older woman all in black and bedecked in a twinkle of silver bracelets and rings that clattered as she moved, as if they might have been there to remind her of her own existence with their sound. This was Joyce Blanding, also known around campus as the Widow. She had given her youth to the actor Harry Blanding, thirty years her elder and a local Iowa boy who made good in Hollywood by appearing in a lot of B-movies that never went to video and nobody remembers anymore. A tall, sharp-featured guy who looked like he'd been carved out of a piece of soap, Harry Blanding specialized in playing feisty, grizzled cowboy sidekicks. He dropped dead on the golf course one particularly hot and humid Florida afternoon, and pretty soon after that, the Widow had moved back north, and she was writing and publishing piles of poems and prose vignettes about him and her and all the sordid ins and outs of their life as together as one. Not quite Sylvia Plath and Ted Hughes, but close.

Emily joined them, and Deek made the introduction. The Widow lifted her chin, perked her ears, listening and sniffing the air around her. Emily was so polite. She was such a lady. She was smiling sweetly, maybe even a little bit wistfully, at a woman who could not see her, and when she spoke, "Very nice to meet you, dear," she raised her voice as if the deficiency were an aural rather than a visual one.

Deek explained that they had been discussing the Widow's latest work, which she had already described as a collection of dreams, featuring her late husband. Emily leaned forward, shouting, "You must have loved him very much!" The Widow's eyes rolled up, swimming in a milk blue goo.

This was at a time when a whole slew of books were being published and then quickly exposed as being more creative than academic and more fiction than non. Everybody was talking about it, some with outrage, some with cynicism, some with sadness, others with glee. The man who had exaggerated his own story of addiction to make himself seem more heroic, the transvestite teenager who turned out to be the invention of a middle-aged woman who ran a boarding house in Utah, the newspaper reporter who had concocted a whole series of magazine articles about a non-existent corporation and its Ponzi profits that had bankrupted a whole town of gullible investors somewhere in Illinois.

"Well," Deek was saying, "I think it's all a crock. Pure bullshit." His voice was loud, deep, rolling, and it turned some heads. He took the Widow's hand, pulled her close, shook her, and she chimed.

Emily looked confused. "Oh, but I thought that's what stories were supposed to be. Made up, I mean. That's why they're stories, isn't it? Because they're not true?" She looked around for help. "Or have I got it all wrong again?"

This from the woman who wrote *Forevermore*, which in our humble opinion is one of the most beautiful stories ever told.

"Sentimental crap," is what Fabricunt called it.

"A shamelessly treacled romance," according to the supercilious Peregrine Phillips.

All you have to do to know that they were both wrong is read the jacket flap: "A sweeping romance rendered with breathtaking artistry and emotional depth, *Forevermore* captures the beauty and pain of married life, revealing in layer after layer of richly observed detail and exquisitely rendered prose a world that blends the mundane and the mysterious, the familiar and the fantastic, the normal and the numinous." (Numinous: supernatural, mysterious, divine.)

The Widow's bracelets clattered as the raised her hand. "But," she said, "there's truth and then there's Truth!" You'd have to see it written down in order to understand what she meant by this, but Deek got the point. His grin was amazed. He put an arm around her shoulder and shook her so her breasts wobbled and her jewelry chimed. "Brilliant," he said. "Genius."

Some people were tittering. The fluffed up slut who looked like a stripper in her fringed green dress, her platform shoes, her big glass beads, her black and blue tats. The pimply wallflower with the chewed fingernails, chapped lips, scars on the insides of her thighs. A farm fresh blonde in her pastel sweater set and pearls. The grease-ball dork with pens in his pocket. The side-burned skinhead in his crumpled clothes. These were the students who came to Springer to learn about the world. As self-absorbed and ignorant as alley cats.

"Don't you know who he is?" Mollie shouted at them. "And her! Don't you recognize her? She's the author of *Forevermore*, the best book that was ever written!" (At least, that's what she wishes she had said.)

Emily had excused herself and was tottering off through the crowd again, skewered chicken still in hand. There was nothing more to say. Deek had finished his champagne, and he turned away, too, on a mission to find more. And so, there stood the Widow; like the cheese, she was alone.

Of course, Emily had already figured out about

the shoes. She'd seen the others looking at her and at Deek; she'd heard the hiss of whispers, didn't have to guess at what was being said. Deek's first response was to try and cheer her up. Those people at the party, what did they know? Had they ever been their friends, really? Nothing but bunch of ego-maniacal ignoramuses, he snorted. "There's truth, and then there's Truth! Bah!" And Mollie had to agree with him there, piping up from her place in the back seat of the Lincoln like a choir responding to the calls of a Baptist preacher: "That's right!" "You got it!" "You tell 'em!" "Amen!"

But Emily wouldn't be that easily cheered. "They think I'm a doddering old fool," she said, standing in her driveway there in her stocking feet, holding the offending shoes in her hands, evidence of her incompetence, *non compos mentis*. Mollie made an attempt to shoulder the blame for it herself because she was the one who was supposed to be looking after her, but Emily wouldn't hear it. "You can't do everything, dear," she said. "And if I can't even be trusted to put on my own clothes properly..."

Deek put his arm around her, and that's when he noticed that her dress was misbuttoned, too. He scowled at Mollie, then turned Emily around and began to fix it for his her.

"Emily, my girl," he said, "you *are* a doddering

old fool." He turned her to face him again. "And me, I'm a decrepit old crank, aren't I? I thought you knew that of us."

She frowned. "It's not a joke, Deek."

He responded with a sigh. "No, I don't suppose it is." Then, "Maybe we should call it quits, Emily."

"Quits?"

He nodded. "Take matters into our own hands, while we still can. Before somebody else decides to do it for us."

"Oh…" Her eyes were wide.

Mollie's welled with tears, blurring things prettily.

Deek said, "I think I've had enough, don't you?"

"Enough of what?" Mollie asked, but Deek ignored her so effectively she might not have been there at all. She persisted: "Enough of what!?" Plato was inside the kitchen, whining and scratching at the back door.

Deek turned to Mollie finally, and his smile was nothing less than beatific. He raised his hands, spread his arms, closed his eyes, tipped his chin, lifted his face to the sky. "Enough of all of this..."

What exactly was it that Deek was suggesting? Mollie would be left to wonder. Carbon monoxide in the closed garage? Plastic bags, sleeping pills, vodka? Oven gas, hangman's rope, razor blades, gun? (She insists that she never thought of poison.) (Honestly, that possibility never crossed her mind.)

Before Emily could speak, Deek put a finger to her lips. She turned back toward the house, but he and Mollie lingered in the drive.

She didn't know what to say. His smile was pained. Her whites, in the sunshine, were blindingly bright. The world was steaming after the rains. Green grass, and the roses blood red. The screen door slapped shut behind Emily. Bees buzzed. Mosquitoes whined. Deek slapped at the back of his neck, looked at his palm, then at Mollie. (To tell the truth, she was craving a cigarette.) (And at the back of her mind the memory of Doyle Hirleman's blue eyes burned.)

"Well, sir…," she began. She noticed the sweat that was beading on his temples, sliding down into the creases in his neck. Her own armpits were damp and itching. (That synthetic uniform fabric did not breathe.)

He was staring at her, studying her, as if she were a stranger and he was wondering what she was doing there. He blinked. Tilted his head one way, then the other. His face was blank. She noticed the tiny tremble in the hand that held his cane.

"Deek, are you all right?"

He took a step back. His face had gone pale, his

lips livid, and the muddy lentigines on his cheeks and brow seemed to deepen and spread. She guided him closer to the house, into the shade where it was cooler. "Can I get you something? A glass of water? Do you want to sit down?"

He was leaning on her now, his face was close to hers, his nose was in her hair, but when she recoiled from the bog-smell of his breath, he stiffened, reached for her, his hand gripped her arm, and he pulled her back.

"What exactly are your intentions, Mollie?" he asked and gave her a little shake.

"Intentions?" Her heart was pounding. She could feel the color filling her face. He was watching her closely, which only made it worse.

"For your life," he said. "What are your plans? Your dreams. Your ambitions. What do you want to do? Who would you like to be? When you grow up."

Hardly anybody ever asked her these kinds of questions anymore. They used to, once upon a time, when she was younger and still thought of as gifted, but it didn't take much to figure out that what they were calling "gifted" back home in Nowhere was called "normal" everyplace else, and the truth is that for the last year or so of high school Mollie had pretty much stopped working or even showing up for classes anymore, with the result that everybody pretty much stopped expecting great things from her anymore either. They figured she'd already hit her own ceiling, it seemed, and she herself didn't disagree. All promise, no product. That looked like it was going to be her story. Mr. Mifflin had made it clear that he thought that all that potential was wasted in a girl anyway, and his wife had never had any great expectations for their younger daughter beyond that she would grow up, go away, and leave them in peace, which by that time Mollie had already accomplished. She had graduated from high school the spring before, and when she left town most everybody who knew her would have had to admit—if they were asked and if they even noticed her absence at all—that they didn't miss her much. (Everybody except her one and only and best friend Postscript, that is.)

Nowhere is a working class town and, as such, the folks there don't put a lot of faith in higher education, especially not if it means reading a lot of books—which Mollie did—and double-especially not if those books are novels or poetry or anything else that carries with it the self-indulgent stink of "art." Those people tend to believe it's better if you're planning to do something practical with your life—like fixing cars or passing out parking tickets or adding up numbers or having babies—like them.

Mollie shakes herself free. Deek wobbles, but doesn't fall. She tells him that she doesn't know about the future, but she is very happy with things the way they were just then, in the present.

"You can't stay here forever," he says.

This shocks her. Is he going to ask her to leave? Is that what this is about? Because of a meatloaf without meat?

"I'm sorry," she begins. "I never meant to… If it's the meatloaf…"

He snorts, shakes his head. No, that isn't it at all. She has her whole life ahead of her. She should be considering a course for it. She should be in school. She should be making friends. She should have a boyfriend. She should go out and enjoy herself, while she still can, while she's still young. And now his look seems wistful.

She told him the truth then (for once), which was that she didn't know what she wanted to do. They had been going along all summer, and everybody was happy, she thought, so why make waves? Live in the moment, don't worry about tomorrow, that sort of thing.

He asked her whether she had any special talents

that she wanted to develop. Other than cooking, that is. He smiled.

She said, no, she didn't. Not that she knew of anyway. She didn't tell him about the mind-reading. Mind-scripting, it was. That was a secret talent, not to be mentioned, not to be shared. It wasn't fully developed yet, anyway.

"Maybe you'll get married. Find some good--looking young man and settle down and have a family..."

Mollie had to smirk at this. "Do I look like a housewife to you, Mr. Molene?"

He regarded her closely then—took in her spiked hair, tongue stud, nose ring, the bracelet of heart tattoos encircling her wrist. Shook his head, sighed. No. Not a housewife.

"Show business maybe," he said. "You look like one of those kids on TV. Can you act?"

(Could she act. Ha.)

Deek had been having conversations like this with young women for most of his life, of course. As founder of the Springer College Creative Writing Program, he had taught and counseled thousands of them as they passed through his and Emily's purview.

"Couldn't I be a writer?" Mollie was asking. "Like Emily? Like you?"

He squinted doubtfully and sucked on his teeth. Then, "Sure," he said. "Why not? Stranger things have happened, I suppose."

So sure, all right, we're not afraid to say it: bringing out the goblets was all Mollie's idea. A second-to--last resort, you could say. She'd found them up in the attic when she was rummaging through the Emily's old things, which was maybe wrong of her, but she couldn't help it; her curiosity got the better of her, and she didn't mean any harm, she had no intention of taking anything for herself. (And if there are people who want to say that anything was missing, how are they ever going to be able to prove that's true?) Everybody who knows Mollie knows how much she loves a good garage sale, and there was all this stuff up there; she couldn't keep her hands off it, though she did her best, for a while, at first. Living in that attic was like having a permanent estate sale—the best kind, when you get there first thing in the morning before anybody else, and it's all spread out on the dewy lawn and in the driveway, on tables and blankets, with little pieces of tape marking the prices.

The goblets were in a nondescript brown box, wrapped in a *Chicago Tribune* from February, 1959, and they were as perfect and complete as Mollie had ever imagined them to be, when she first read *Forevermore*.

FOREVERMORE

by
Emily Molene

Chapter Two

The storm was over now, and Alice was sleeping. Leo lay on his back, listening to the rainwater dripping from the eaves and the gentle sound of her breathing, like waves upon a distant shore, until another noise caught his attention. He held his own breath, and there it was again: a tinkle of glass, whispers, soft moaning. Was there someone else in the room with them?

He sat up quickly and looked around, but there didn't seem to be anyone there. A dream, maybe? He noticed the goblets on the table and thought again of the price that Alice had paid for them. She was going to have to learn to be more careful with their money in the future. He would have to teach her how to manage it if they were to get by on what he was likely to earn as an academic and an author, as they'd planned.

Alice had been so sure about those goblets, completely unable to resist her sudden impulse to buy them, although they had seemed quite ordinary to him. What was it about them that had so enchanted her? He glanced at her again, sleeping peacefully, then got up from the bed and crossed the room to have a look at them again.

The fluted bowls lay on the table, missing their stems. He was angry. They'd cost so much, and now they appeared to be broken. He picked up one of the bowls and cradled it in his palm. Nearby was its stem, misshapen somehow. Leo looked closer to see that it was not just one after all, but both, the man and the woman, and they seemed to be clasped together in an embrace, squirming in each other's arms.

They were alive? The small woman saw Leo, and she pushed the small man away. He turned and saw, too, that Leo was watching them.

"Well, well, well," he said. "It's about time."

Leo frowned. Rubbed his eyes. Was he dreaming? "You're real?"

The small woman stood up. "Well of course, we're real." She turned to her companion. "Did you hear that? He wants to know are we real."

"I heard him. I'm not deaf you know."

The woman stretched, stood, arched her back. "It feels good to be able to move again."

In the bed, Alice stirred. "Leo? Who are you talking to?"

He didn't know what to say.

She got out of bed and crossed the room to him. "What is it?" She looked at him, then at the table. When she saw the small people, she gasped. She peered closer. "They're alive," she said.

The small woman snorted. "Another genius," she said.

The small man walked over to the edge of the tabletop, where he sat down. "Okay, here's the deal. You've got one wish. You make it, we grant it, you get what you want, we've done our job, everybody's happy, simple and plain." He brushed his hands together. Fini.

The small woman scolded him. "You're going too fast. Slow down."

"Oh, they heard me. It's not that hard." He turned to Alice and Leo. "So, what'll it be?" Alice frowned. "What'll what be?"

The small woman nodded. "I told you. See? You went too fast. You always go too fast. You have to take your time, relax, give them a chance to catch their breath."

The small man ignored her and glared at Alice, impatiently. "A wish, lady. A wish. Get it? How hard is that?"

"I think he wants you to make a wish," Leo said.

"See, it's like this...," the small woman began. She moved closer to Leo, came to the edge of the table top, looked down, reeled a bit and stepped back.

The small man scoffed. "She's afraid of heights," he said.

The small woman was looking up at Leo. "Maybe you could just..." She gestured, a lifting motion with both hands. "...hold me?"

The small man smirked. "Cheap thrill."

"Go on, Leo," Alice said.

He reached out and the small woman climbed into the pocket of his palm. She clasped his thumb, holding on for dear life.

"Ooh! Not too fast now."

Leo was peering at the woman in his palm. She went on with her explanation.

"Okay," she said, "it's like this. We're magic, see? You have to ask us for a wish, and we have to grant it. Like that. Get it?"

"A wish? What kind of a wish?"

"Anything at all, sweetie. Whatever your little heart desires. Money. Fame. Fortune. You name it, it's yours."

"Success?" Leo asked.

The small woman smiled. "Sure, we do success." She turned to look down at the small man. "Don't we?"

He was pacing back and forth on the tabletop. "Let's see... success... success... sure, why not?"

"Okay, then I wish..." Leo began, but Alice grabbed his arm to stop him.

"No, wait!"

The small woman almost tumbled out of his jostled hand.

Alice winced. "Oh, I'm sorry," she said. "But Leo, you can't make a wish."

"Why not?"

The little man shivered with exasperation. "Yeah, why not?"

Alice lowered her voice. "Because it's a trick."

The little woman leaned over the edge of Leo's palm and shouted down to the small man. "She says it's a trick."

The small man stomped his feet and waved his arms around. "Well of course it's a trick. What, do you think something like this happens every day?"

"What are you talking about, honey?" Leo asked.

"The wish. It's a trick. They get you to ask for something, and then when you get it, you realize you didn't want it after all. Or the price you have to pay for it is more than you expected, or the wish you made wasn't precise enough and so you get the opposite of what you really wanted. It's in all the fairy tales."

The small woman wheedled, "Oh no, we're not like that. Really. I promise."

Leo put her back down on the table and stepped back. "What am I doing? I can't believe this. This can't be happening. I'm dreaming, right? Either that or I'm crazy. Or drunk. Crazy drunk and dreaming. What was in that brandy, Alice? Absinthe?"

With that, he went over to the bed, climbed in and pulled the covers up to his chin.

On the tabletop, the small woman scolded the small man. "Oh great. You scared him."

"*I* scared him? You were the one up there rubbing yourself against his thumb like some kind of a shameless—"

"Don't you say it. Don't you dare."

"Or what?"

"Just don't. I mean it. I'm warning you."

"Ha! You're warning me? What're you gonna do? Twist my arm? Beat me up? Break my leg? Go ahead then. Just try it. I dare ya. Come on. Hit me right here, go ahead."

He stuck out his jaw for her. The small woman

balled up her hands into fists and flailed at him, but he ducked away, and she missed. She regained her balance and threw herself upon him in a fury.

Alice went over to the bed. "Leo? Are you all right?" But his eyes were closed, and he seemed to be asleep. She sat on the edge of the mattress. She traced the outline of his cheek with her fingertip.

His eyes opened. "Alice?"

He reached for her, and she crawled into his arms.

On the tabletop, the small man and small woman continued to wrestle. She had him in a headlock, and he was struggling to get free. "Take it back. Say you're sorry," she said. He strained against her. "Never!"

He flipped her onto her back and pinned her, but his movements were slower now, more stiff.

The small woman winced. "Ooh, that hurts."

"Of course it hurts. It's supposed to hurt."

Outside the wind picked up, and the downpour began again.

"Let me go."

"First, say you're sorry."

"Why should I?"

"Just say it."

"Make me."

"I'm making you. Here, how do you like this?"

"Ow! Let go of me right now."

The arguing voices rose, mingled, and were lost in the loud rush of pouring rain.

Soon the small man and woman were what they had been before, nothing more than a pair of goblets on a table in a hotel room in Paris. She was tipped over, and she lay on her side in a puddle of spilled brandy. He was standing, and his fluted bowl was half full.

While in the bed across the room, the exhausted newlyweds slept.

Chapter Four

The Grotto was a favorite spot for Springer students, on Main Street, in the windowless cellar of an old office building—very Bohemian, with beaded curtains, low tables, velvety sofas and hefty chairs, concrete floor, raw cement walls with all the pipes exposed—and that night it was jam-packed with people, as everybody was back from summer break and summer jobs, ready to party before the semester seriously kicked in. Binge drinkers slamming back Jager shots at the bar. DJ spinning vinyl in a booth. Even a mirror ball, throwing out snowflakes of light over a mostly empty dance floor, but the night was young.

When Mollie arrived Doyle was sitting at a corner table, and it looked like he was waiting there just for her, although he was in the shadows and so it was hard to tell for sure whether his smile was one of expectation or surprise.

She had to make a decision about whether to let him in on the fact that she wasn't old enough to even be in a bar this late without her parents (ha ha), much less drink in one, because she also had the fake ID that Postscript had procured for her—Emily Molene, his joke—and it was good enough to at least have gotten her in through the chaos at the door.

She was thinking that honesty might be the best policy, for once—anybody who has ever seen a TV sitcom knows that you don't want to get a new relationship off on the wrong foot by basing it on a lie—and yet it didn't seem so smart to tell him the *whole* truth, so she only gave him half, and honestly, that seemed plenty generous to her. That is, she admitted that she was too young to drink legally, but she also said she'd turned nineteen the previous spring when actually she would only be eighteen in October. (Or something like that.) At first, he just smiled harder at her, as if he'd already suspected as much, and then he squinted at her sideways, like he was trying to figure out whether even that was the truth. What, she thought, afraid of a little jailbait? He was drinking beer (PBR), and she asked for a Diet Coke with lime, and then she was so nervous that she drank it fast and he got her another one, which then had her thrumming, tapping her foot and drumming her fingers and yammering on about anything and everything that came into her head—blah-blah-blah and yackety-yak-yak--yak.

He offered her a cigarette (Marlboro), smiled again, seemed genuinely glad to have her there with him, and so she was on her best behavior. He told her some more about who he was, and she told him some more about herself—a little bit of get-to-know-you--better, all very civilized and grownup and polite.

She'd changed out of her uniform and into one of Emily's old outfits—an almost perfect pink and grey mohair sweater with cropped sleeves and pearl buttons and only one moth hole in it that she could see, black silk pedal pushers, leather ballet flats with bows on the toes. Except for her spiky hair and the nose piercing and the stud in her tongue and the tattoo on her wrist, she looked like a 1950s co-ed ready to hop into her greaseball boyfriend's souped-up Chevy to go drag racing on a dirt road between cornfields under a full moon somewhere. Real Natalie Wood. Although Doyle didn't exactly fit that James Dean part. He looked more like an overworked waiter who had missed a few showers and slept in his clothes.

He told her that he was only working for the catering company part time to pay the bills, while in his real life he was a filmmaker. He was not a Springer student either, but a townie, born and raised in Brevity, and he had no connection to the college and no plan to stay there for the rest of his life, no intention of falling in with his parents and his brothers and his old friends who were every one of them going nowhere fast. He had his own camera, he said, and he wanted to go to film school someday in California or New York (somewhere!), but in the meantime he'd been putting together a few short films of his own, mostly shoot-em-ups based on the videogames that he'd played all through high school, using his friends and family as (unpaid) actors. She asked him if his films were any good, and he shrugged and answered, "Maybe," which made her appreciate his honesty and his humility, both. Then he brought his hands up to his eyes and framed her face in the rectangle of his forefingers and thumb. "I bet you'll be very photogenic," he said to her. She noticed that his hands were long and slim, and his fingernails were clean.

Like Deek, Doyle wanted to know what Mollie had planned for her life. Now everybody was asking her this, it seemed. She thought an actress sounded nice, as Deek had suggested, but she told Doyle that what she really wanted to do was save the world, feed the hungry, bring peace to the planet. She sounded like a beauty pageant contestant, he said, but she was serious. She asked him, "If you could wish for anything, what would it be?" He went through the usual list. Everybody does that first—money, health, love, time—those are the big ones or all the various permutations thereof. But what if you wanted to save the world? Be a hero? What then? What would do it? Food for everyone? Happiness? Freedom? Peace? This is what they talked about, and that's how she knew that he was the one for her.

In turn, Mollie gave Doyle a cautiously generalized bit of backstory of her own. That she was born and raised in Nowhere, New York. That Nowhere is a small town in what has been called the Burned-Over District of the state. That the Burned-Over District is an area in central and western New York, home to an unusual number of spiritualists, millennialists, and utopians, and so named after the Second Great Awakening because by then the place had been so heavily evangelized during antebellum revivalism that there was no more fuel in the way of unbelievers left over to burn, or convert. A hotbed of religious fervor, the district spawned not only an inordinate number of ordinary congregations of mainline Protestants but also many more innovative (and dangerous) religious movements including the Latter Day Saints, the Millerites, the Shakers, the Oneida Society, and those notorious Fox sisters of Hydesville, who conducted the first table-rapping séances in the area, which led to the Spiritualists who were centered in Lilydale, where Mollie's aunt Lucy Skye, neeé Miller, practiced her psychic craft of communicating with the dead.

Whether this creeped Doyle out or intrigued him was hard to tell. Mollie did her best to normalize it by bringing in her painfully down-to-earth and ordinary family—her mother and father, along with her sister who was married to the cop and had one kid already and another one on the way. Mollie made it sound all nice and tidy. Mom works in the accounting department of a large pediatrics group, and Dad is an actuary.

"What's that?"

"A professional wet blanket." Big grin, all teeth. Ha ha.

He didn't ask her what she was doing in Brevity. Most likely he just assumed that she was a student. A freshman, wet behind the ears, looking after a couple of helpless old geezers in exchange for her room and board. Well, that was close. She had taken that one creative writing class with Dr. Phillips over the summer. And she had gone to a reading and lecture delivered by Fabricunt at the public library downtown.

Once they'd made it past the basics, Doyle and Mollie talked some more about this and that, everything and nothing, but when the music started playing again, a slow ballad, then he paused and stood up and gave her the once-over, twice-over with those smashed glass blue eyes. His mouth had a way of naturally curling up at the corners as if he was always smiling, quietly amused at something, himself maybe. He put out one of his long slender clean hands and pulled Mollie to her feet, drew her close. And so they danced, their bodies a perfect fit, the snowfall from the mirror ball drifting over then… and then, when he kissed her, all sound stopped and time froze… and there they were, the two of them together, poised on the brink of eternity…

Okay, that's not how it was. Call it wishful thinking. What really happened is they talked for a while and then they were joined by a woman who plopped herself down right beside Doyle, so close that she was practically in his lap. This turned out to be the photographer from the party, and she introduced herself as Elizabeth Wendler "But-everybody--calls-me Mouse"—from Linwood, Iowa, in her last year at Springer, majoring in business and minoring in English lit, studying in weekly workshops with both Dr. Phillips and Fabricunt with a little bit of photography and art on the side. A lesbian, it turned out, and so there wasn't anything between her and Doyle, not that that mattered. And the slut in the green dress? That was Mouse's ex-girlfriend; her name was Sybil, and over the summer she'd changed her emphasis from fiction to poetry as well as from women to men. Just like that, she had declared herself postmodern and straight and moved out of Mouse's apartment and into a room of her own.

So Doyle was introducing Mollie to Mouse, who was grinning at her in a goofy, friendly way, shaking her hand and shouting over the din, something about "fucking poets," but Mollie didn't have enough context to be able to tell whether she was using the word as an adjective or a verb, cursing the genre or suggesting something else that might be done with its practitioners because just then her attention was distracted by a big ruckus at the door as another group from Dr. Phillips's party barged into the bar. Fabricunt was in the lead, elbowing through the crowd to a setup in the back corner, where she claimed her territory. This was the official Springer Creative Writing Program's space, Mouse explained, so designated by Deek Molene himself back in the days when he was still the one who was in charge of it all.

The students who had been sitting there cleared out obediently and immediately to make room for the famous scribblers—Fabricunt and the Widow and Dr. Phillips, plus Sybil in the green dress, the wallflower and the milkmaid, the skinhead and the dork, as well as John and Sarah Steele.

Mollie noticed that Fabricunt was all over John, and Sarah had this pretty, pained smile on her face as she eyed the two of them together. It looked like everybody was either drunk already or well on their way to it, except for Sarah Steele. She was sitting in the corner, perched on the seat of a turquoise leather chair, and she was so pretty and sweet that it was as if there were a halo on her, shining down just so from a yellow bulb in the overhead light.

Meanwhile, Mouse and Doyle seemed to have picked up where they'd apparently last left off, pointedly ignoring the others, snubbing the ex and jumping right into the thick of an argument about film and books or some such intellectual college poppycock—with so much intensity that pretty soon they had both forgotten all about Mollie, too, so she ducked in and started helping herself to their pitcher of beer. If you can't beat 'em, you know what you have to do.

When Mollie looked again, it was to see that Dr. Phillips had made his move and was leading Sarah

Steele out onto the dance floor while Mouse's ex had managed to edge out Fabricunt to find her own way into the arms of John.

What Mollie didn't tell Doyle that night at the Grotto was the whole sad story of her lonely childhood. (Boo-hoo.) Such as the part about the grey bleak day in March when she was born, brought forth into the world just a few moments ahead of the small dark corpse of her twin brother, who was to have been named Horace, after his grandfather on the Miller side, a direct descendent of William Miller, whose predictions for the end of the world had failed in 1844, creating for his followers—known as the Millerites—an event called the Great Disappointment, which then went on to beget a few new whacked out apocalyptic sects, including first the Seventh Day Adventists and then later the Branch Davidians, who were so famously inflagrated by the FBI in their compound at Waco, Texas, along with their criminally misguided leader David Koresh in 1993.

Nor the part about how Horace was the son Mollie's father always wanted but never had, caught up as he'd been in the coils of his sister's umbilical cord, strangled by it (by her?) at twenty-six weeks but carried to term by their heroic mother in order to preserve Mollie, the second daughter, the one they never wanted but now had, a great disappointment of their own.

Nor the part about her sister, six years older and in and out of trouble, involved in things Mollie was too young to have more than only a vague inkling of at the time—sex and drugs and rock and roll, all of it too predictable to be interesting to anybody but herself.

Nor the part about her mother, that black hole of narcissistic self-regard, an infinite feedback loop of self-reflection.

Nor the part about her dad, a free-flowing fountain of bad news, overworked and underappreciated and depressed.

Mollie didn't tell Doyle any of this. Not about her earliest childhood memories, either, spent watching mad Aunt Lucy talking to the dead as she conducted séances at $50 a head in her dark apartment on the nights when Mollie's mother had left her there in her care. Lucy tucked Mollie in the back bedroom while she did her work with her clients, talking by way of table rappings and trances and Ouija boards to their deceased loved ones—all the dead husbands and wives, sisters, brothers, mothers, fathers, lovers, even cats and dogs and, one time, a parrot. Lucy Miller was only one of many mediums who lived and worked in Lilydale, so she had a lot of competition, and as with everything else, it all came down to advertising, which had Mollie standing outside on the street corner with a sign: "Talk to your dead ones…"—and an arrow—"…here."

When she was eight years old, Mollie's dead brother began to talk to her himself. Just whispers in the dark at first—a voice in her head, calling out her name. Or sometimes it would be laughter, sometimes a whistle. She knew it was him, who else could it be? "Mollie! Mollie!" This frightened her at first, but soon she was used to it, and then she was grateful for it, in a way. She found it comforting, not to be alone, to have him always there with her.

How could he talk, though? Was he growing up, just like Mollie, in some other parallel world where she had died and he had not? Or was he still a fetus, curled up on himself like a worm, floating in an amniotic limbo on the other side of the thin membrane that separates this dimension of the living from that one of the dead? Mollie didn't know, and she knew better than to ask. Just the mention of his name sent her mother into a black funk out of which her hand might fly fast enough to smack Mollie if she wasn't watchful and quick enough to dodge away.

Mollie didn't tell Doyle, either, about being alone and on her own most of the time, left to her own devices, hanging around Nowhere, coming and going pretty much as she pleased. She'd had no friends because she didn't want them. She had Horace, after all. So she preferred to be left alone, and she didn't exactly fit in anyway—not pretty enough to be popular, not athletic, not dopey enough to be a geek, but not a stoner either. Sure, there were plenty of kids who looked like her, the ones who smoked pot behind the school and got into all kinds of trouble with drinking and drugs—car wrecks and overdoses and fistfights and even a knifing or a shooting or a house set on fire every now and then. Those kids were bored! But not Mollie. She kept to herself, and so they were not her friends. She figured her sister had got herself into enough trouble for both of them, and she didn't want to be like Janet in any way, not if she could possibly help it. Truth is, Mollie was more a poser than anything. She dressed as if she were a part of that scene, but she never was, not really. It was just her way of protecting herself, we could say, and probably some psychologist would have a heyday with all of it, how Mollie did everything she could think of to keep everybody else at bay.

What else didn't Mollie tell Doyle? About Rocky Point Park and the old haunted house that was there, where she liked to hang out by herself when things got too cold and dark and dead at home. It was a rundown, abandoned Blair Witch kind of place, too spooky to be alone in at night but okay during the day, and she went there often, to get away from everybody, because if she stayed too close to home, then her father would start thinking he had to find something for her to do. Or her mother would cook up something to blame her for doing. Or for not doing. Or for doing all wrong.

About how she was at that house minding her own business, reading this book that she'd found at a tag sale—because that was her hobby then: tag sales and church sales and rummage sales. Digging through the piles of other people's junk. She never ceased to be amazed at what you could buy for next to nothing that way.

About this kid who came stumbling in, drunk on the gas fumes he'd inhaled from the pump over at the 7-Eleven on Elm. He was on his own then, too, even more so than Mollie had ever been, abandoned by his helpless dad and cruel stepmom, who kept locking him out of their big fancy house up on Crescent Hill to teach him a lesson, they said, although just exactly what that lesson was supposed to be was never totally clear—to him or to them either. He was just a kid, a couple of years younger than Mollie, and he had three older sisters, much older, by ten years at least, which made him the late-comer to the family—an afterthought, a postscript—and then his mother died of some kind of cancer when he was only six and his father married the Demon soon after that, but she hated him and the dad didn't know what to do about that, so there it was. They made it their business to punish him for every little thing that went wrong until he had no choice but to run away altogether if he was going to get half his fair chance to survive in this world.

Stupid stuff, like if he didn't make his bed or if he forgot to put his plate in the dishwasher. For that, they'd make him get down on his hands and knees to scrub the dirt out of the cracks at the edges of the kitchen floor with a toothbrush. Or if he said anything that sounded like he might be talking back at her, she'd slap a strip of duct tape over his mouth. If he complained about his homework, they'd tie him to a post in the back yard until he'd finished it, even if it was late, even if it was dark, even if it was cold.

But he was a regular Houdini, that kid, and no matter what they did, he'd still figure out some way to break free and wander off because eventually they always forgot about him out there anyway.

His real name was Paul Solomon, but his tag was Postscript or P.S., and he was just this poor sweet scrawny kid with a rat's nest of messy black curls on his head and scabs and scars all over his arms and legs, and he never hurt anybody but himself. We can sincerely attest to that as well as to the fact that he did not deserve any of what those monsters did to him, but he never gave in to them either, and you just have to have some kind of respect for that, no matter what else happens.

Mollie didn't tell Doyle, either, about how she'd bought this box of old paperbacks from a driveway over on Birch Street from some sad old man who was just trying to unload some of his dead wife's stuff. Breast cancer—and she'd put up a good fight, so it had taken her long enough to shuffle off her mortal coil that she'd collected a good pile of magazines and trashy books and one-thousand-piece jigsaw puzzles for giving her something else to do while she waited for the end. He was selling off all her clothes and shoes and cheap jewelry and cosmetics, too, which was maybe slightly disgusting and mercenary of him, but there were also a bunch of paperback books in a blue plastic milk crate that Mollie bought for more than she should have paid (ten dollars) on account of she felt sorry for the guy and so she just couldn't bring herself to haggle with him the way she normally would have done, not with him standing there all gray and slack and silent, as if somebody had come along and knocked right out of him the last good breath of air he'd ever have again. The spines were cracked and broken and the covers were torn and some of the pages had come loose, but the books were still just as full of words as they'd ever been, so, so what? That's the point, isn't it? She did slip him one of Lucy's cards, thinking that maybe a session with her might cheer him up somewhat. Whether he followed through on it, though, she would never know.

Mollie didn't tell Doyle about how in that crate there was one book that was special, a storytelling wonder that she found only after she'd already slogged through the soft melodrama of half the others. This was *Forevermore* by Emily Molene. She picked it up one idle afternoon, and then she couldn't put it down until it was done. By the time she got to Brevity, Mollie had read it at least ten times over again or more. Although you could say that the whole premise is a little bit cheesy and dumb, as Postscript and Mollie both agreed after they got to know each other and she told him the story: about how this woman named Alice buys a pair of magic goblets and then even though she can have anything she wants—anything!—she loves her children so much that she saves her own once-in-a-lifetime wish for them. Who does that? Not Mollie's parents, and not Postscript's either. (Yours?)

On the cover of the book, there was a painting of the goblets themselves with their fluted bowls and human stems and inside the back flap, a photograph of the esteemed author herself. This was a visage that Mollie kept turning to again and again—that pretty young face so open and sweet, her smile shy, her eyes kind and brimming with what looked like tenderness and understanding and a mother's unconditional and never-ending love.

Mollie didn't tell Doyle either about how she was talking to Postscript about this book and about the woman who wrote it, and she was showing him the picture and saying, "I'd like to know her," and he was laughing at her, saying "Look at the date, you asshole. She'd be an old lady by now. For sure. she doesn't look like that anymore."

But Mollie was determined to find Emily Molene anyway, and maybe Postscript's mocking her just made her that much more intent on it than ever.

She tried to call the publisher, but they must have long ago gone out of business because nobody had ever heard of them, and when she called a bunch of other publishers, just randomly, they all said they'd never heard of Emily Molene either. How could that be? She'd written a book; didn't that make her famous?

Mollie checked down at the library, too, but they didn't know anything about anything there either. At which point Postscript told her to forget about it, and for a while she took his advice and did.

Mollie told Doyle Hirleman none of this.

But then, like in a good story—though this was not a story, this was Mollie's life, this was real—it all came to a head at once, when on the very day of her graduation from high school, she found out where Emily Molene was. This bit of information came from a listing in an old compendium of published authors, a Who's Who so far out of date that it had been relegated to a back shelf of the library and then put out for sale on a rummage table, where Postscript found it and bought it and then gave it to Mollie as a graduation present. Okay, he didn't buy it, he stole it, but that is really neither here nor there because he would have bought it if he'd had the money, and if he hadn't stolen it, nobody would have bought it anyway; it would have been thrown out with the garbage and burned or added to the landfill and then taken centuries to turn back into dirt again. Therefore, that he had it and that he gave it to Mollie was just as well and even better. Or so she told him.

He'd marked the page with a rose that he picked from the church garden, and there it was: Emily Molene, author of one novel: *Forevermore*. Born Emily Fairchild in Linwood, Iowa, 1924. Married author Deacon Bensenhaver Molene twenty-five years later. And on the previous page: Deek himself. His bibliography was much longer, of course. Current position: Springer College, Department of English, Creative Writing Program, Director. Where was Springer? Postscript shrugged. How would he know, he'd never been out of Nowhere, and neither had she.

Brevity, Iowa, as it turned out.

And then when Mollie came back home later that very same day—well, actually it was night because before that there had been some of the usual celebrating that went on after the graduation ceremony—when she came home, there was all her stuff lying out in the front yard as if she might have been having a sale of her own, which of course she wasn't. Not to her knowledge anyway. Her mother was sitting there in the dark on the front stoop, smoking cigarettes and drinking champagne and keeping an eye on her things so that nobody would come by and help themselves, which was decent of her, maybe.

She was having a little celebration of her own, you could say.

Commencement, did Mollie know what that meant? she wanted to know. Sure, it was a long and boring ceremony where the graduates had to wear tasseled hats and sit in the sun listening to a bunch of long and boring speeches about the promise of the future and their responsibility to the world to make it a better place than what they'd found it to be, as if that were possible, the world being the consistently crappy place that it is. Commencement meant she had graduated, and that meant the nightmare that had been her time at high school was finally over. Mrs. Mifflin laughed, took a swig of the champagne—straight from the bottle—crushed out one cigarette (Benson & Hedges 100's DeLuxe Ultra-Light Menthol) and lit another. Blowing smoke, shook her head. Nice try.

"Commencement," she said, suppressing a burp, "is not an ending; it is a beginning."

Prepared for yet another long and boring speech from yet another self-deluded adult with yet another obvious belch of wisdom to impart, Mollie took a seat next to her mother on the stoop. She could see out there on the lawn her collection of stuffed animals and her books and her clothes. Even her shoes. Costume jewelry. Cosmetics. The works.

"Commencement: an act, instance, or time of commencing. Commencing: entering upon. In other words... Beginning."

Silence. The crickets in the grass. The sizzle of the cigarette. The starlight overhead. A distant sound of music, people partying. Dew sparkling on the rounded ears of the pink teddy bear that Dad had won at the fair for Mollie when she was six.

Then: "This is the first day of the rest of our lives, Mollie."

She didn't argue with her. Not day, Mom. Night. It's night. She waited. Then: "*Our* lives?"

More champagne. Another cigarette.

"I thought you quit smoking."

"I did. Now I've started again."

Mollie let this sit.

"We're all going to die," Mom said. Mollie looked at her. Waited. This was going to be one of those nights. When she gets all morose. Too much cancer going around. AIDS. Murder. Ebola. Terror. Bombs and bullets, genocide and war. Nothing make sense anymore. Nothing's what it used to be. Nothing's what it seems. Everything's gone haywire. The world's all gone to hell.

Then: "I've asked your father for a divorce."

And that was the long and the short of it. Mrs.

Mifflin was explaining that she had only stayed with her husband for as long as she did because of her younger daughter, and now that Mollie was finished with high school, there was no reason to keep up any pretense of happiness in a marriage that had been unhappy for a long, long time. Never mind that Mollie was only seventeen. Never mind that she was still a minor. She was being emancipated.

Within a week, Mrs. Mifflin had moved her daughter out of the house, filed for divorce from her husband, and bought a couple of gallons of new paint for Mollie's old bedroom, with the intention of turning it into what was to be her "craft" room. Where she would make the embarrassing needlework shit that she sold at tag sales and church boutiques on the weekends: potholders and toaster covers, trivets and light switch covers, Christmas balls and picture frames. A whole new life, a whole new start. Commencement.

This is what Mollie's mother said to her that night: "It's time for you to go now."

Who knows how long she must have been planning the whole thing, counting off the days until she could be rid of her younger daughter, her great disappointment and her last burden.

Mollie took as much of her stuff as she could carry—clothes, books, and whatnot—and she spent the rest of that night in the haunted house at Rocky Point Park. She could have gone to her sister's instead. Or she might have tried to find her dad and cadge some sympathy from him. She might even have gone to Lilydale and moved in with her Aunt Lucy, gone to work for her. But instead she decided that she would do what her mother wanted her to do: she would commence. Time for her to go now; time to grow up; time to move on. She wrote a note to Postscript, told him to help himself to anything of hers he wanted from the front yard where she'd left it. She used the money that they'd given her for graduation, and she bought a bus ticket to Brevity, Iowa. Just like that, she was off to find her fairy godmother—Emily Molene.

So. That's how it came to be that there was Mollie Mifflin, in a booth in a dark corner near the back of the Grotto that night, and Doyle and Mouse were talking, and Mollie was drinking their beer, and John Steele was dancing with the Ex, and Sarah was in the arms of Dr. Phillips, and he was slobbering all over her, but she still had that beautiful smile on her face and then… well, here's where it gets strange.

Something happens. Maybe it's just the beer plus the one tequila shot that Mollie has had, all of it kicking in at once, but it's like a power surge of some kind, a blinking of the lights maybe, that comes with a poof and a bang, except that the sound is silent, like the voice of Horace in your head. It's more like something that you see than something that you hear, or you smell it or it touches you, and Mollie's looking around but nobody else seems to have noticed this except maybe the blind widow Joyce Blanding, who is all a-jangle, sitting bolt upright in her seat while Fabricunt yammers on about something numbingly unimportant in that cranky loud voice of hers. And Mollie sees, too, that Sarah has suddenly jerked back, startled, from Dr. Phillips' embrace, as if he's goosed her. She's standing there in the middle of the floor blinking while John Steele has the Ex by the shoulders and he's holding her at arm's length, looking at her like she's from another planet, or another dimension, or another galaxy altogether. She hands him a napkin. It appears that his nose is bleeding.

As for Mollie, she's watching this, and she's thinking about the goblets and the wish, about Forevermore and how in it Leo and Alice Bell saved their one wish for their baby, who had not even been conceived yet, that's how much they loved him. That here were two people who would sacrifice every possibility of their own for the sake of the promise of someone else that they loved even more than they loved each other. Except that now she knew the truth, which was that they never did have any children to give their one wish to, and that meant that it was still good, because they hadn't thought to use it, until now.

She interrupted Doyle and Mouse to tell them this, to try to explain it to them, but it was complicated—there was only one wish but you had to have two people to make it, two people who loved each other enough to want exactly the same thing, for themselves and for each other or for somebody else—and maybe it was the beer or maybe it was the tequila, but this came out all garbled, so they were laughing at her, finding it funny, and the more she tried to tell them, the more she tried to get it straight, shouting, "No! I'm serious!" the more tangled up she got and the weirder they thought she was. Exchanged glances, raised eyebrows, indulgent smiles.

"Come on now, Mollie," Mouse said at last, "how about me and Doyle take you home?"

He drove an old white Volvo station wagon, and he was behind the wheel, Mouse was shotgun, and Mollie was in the back seat again like a little kid, but she didn't mind so much this time since she was feeling very sheepish and confused. She couldn't ask them to take her home because then she'd have had to explain that she was living with the Molenes and then they might say something to someone and someone would maybe say it to someone else and pretty soon Deek would be wondering why everybody kept referring to Mollie as the girl who was living with them and then there'd be all kinds of trouble that she'd have to go to great lengths to fix. That's how it works with one lie that builds on another one and then another one builds on that. Plus, she was worrying about how she was going to get into the house without them hearing her. This was the first night she'd ever spent out after dark, and she figured she'd maybe have to bed down in the back seat of the Lincoln again. This actually seemed like a suitable punishment. Little did she know that it was the least of her worries just then.

She told Doyle that she had an apartment not far from there, on Madison and Green, and they could just drop her off at this end of the one-way street rather than having to go all the way around, and they kept asking, "Are you sure you're okay?" and Mollie kept telling them, "Yes! I'm fine." Flashing the famous smile and turning on the charm, full blast. He stopped at the corner, and after an embarrassing fumble with the door handle, she was out and on the sidewalk and careful not to weave. She made her way up the block a ways before ducking into shadow to wait until she was sure the coast was clear and they were good and gone.

It was not a far walk from there, and it was chilly enough on a fall evening to be sobering, so Mollie took her time heading toward the Molenes' house, which loomed big and dark and spooky-looking as ever under a moon that rode a bank of clouds high up in the sky.

As she walked, she began to hear Horace telling her that the time had come for her to stop lying. She had to start telling the truth. He was right. He was always right. That's what he was there for. And so, fully resolved to come clean and do the right thing, she'd explain everything and then ask Deek and Emily to let her actually move in with them for real. She would be good, and she would be responsible. She would really take care of them this time, from there on out. Good care of them. They could count on her. Maybe she could start going to school. Maybe she'd even become a real nurse.

While Mollie was thusly ruminating, a car had turned onto the street in front of her, its headlights flooding the world with light, and she flinched away from it just in time to see and hear and feel something pale and white and ghostly hiss past her, like smoke, into the path of the oncoming vehicle. The driver slammed on the brakes and swerved to avoid the apparition, jumping the curb and shuddering to a stop not more than a tall man's body length away from where Mollie stood. So close, she could feel the warm thrum of heat emanating from its engine and hear the ripples of music playing inside, beyond the tinted windows.

The driver, a woman, was out of the car, and her passenger, a young boy, was right behind her. They both moved quickly, but Mollie was stuck in place. There was the slow-moving smear of the boy's dark hair and the curve of the woman's back as she stopped for a closer look at what was there on the pavement in the middle of the road. She reached out her hand to turn the body over, even as Mollie screamed, "Don't move her!"

The "her" was Emily Molene, and it looked for all the world like she was dead.

Next thing Mollie knew, she was running. Black flats slipping on the sidewalk as she clambered the rest of the way up the hill toward the house. Moonlight flamed in the windows, then went dark again behind the clouds, teasing her, it seemed. At the gate, she stopped and looked back, down at the street. The car. The woman. The boy. Porch lights going on, shadows moving. That white shape in the road.

She hurried around to the side of the house. The Lincoln was there in the driveway, right where Deek had left it earlier, after the party. Mollie stopped at the back door, which was hanging open. Inside, she could see the shadows of the kitchen, dark and still, and the back stairs rising up to the second floor and on beyond, all the way to her own room at the top. She stepped inside, crossed through to the dining room, stood in the silent front hall. She called out, "Deek?" Her voice echoed, plaintive, swallowed whole by the house.

Listen: a soft whimpering sound. The click and whirr of a needle swimming over vinyl. The study door is open. There is a dark shape on the floor. Clouds part again and moonlight streams in to bathe the lifeless-looking body of Deacon Molene in its cold, white, merciless light.

Mollie shrieks. Plato cowers. And then she's found the telephone, and she is dialing out for help.

Forevermore

by

Emily Molene

Chapter Three

The next morning, when Leo awoke, the storm was over, and the room was bright with sunshine. Alice was already up and about, moving back and forth from the closet to the bed, packing her suitcase, ready to go home.

Leo sat up. "How are you feeling?" he asked her.

She came over and kissed him. "Not great. How about you?"

"Little headache is all. Must have been the brandy."

Alice frowned.

"You know," Leo went on, "I had one helluva silly dream last night."

She smiled. "Tell me."

"It was about those damned goblets you bought. They were, I don't know, they started... um, the goblets came to life somehow. And they were talking." He laughed, shook his head.

She looked at the goblets still out on the table. She picked one up, and turned it in the sunlight.

"Pretty wild, huh?"

"Yes," she smiled. "I'll say. Wild."

Two months later, Mr. and Mrs. Leo Bell were home again, and their new life together had begun. Carefully, Alice washed and dried the pair of fanciful goblets that she'd bought in Paris, and she put them on a glass shelf in the dining room, near the window where they could catch the light. She would plant roses in the yard outside. She would turn one of the rooms upstairs into a nursery. There would be a study for Leo, and she'd have a sewing room for herself. The future lay ahead of them, she knew, a whole long life still to come, a bright promise unfolding and unknown. She put her hand on her belly and smiled. She was going to keep the wish. No need to make it now because she already had everything she'd ever wanted. She would save it, for the child, for when the time was right.

So there you have it—what Mollie considered to be the awesome generosity of this woman, who has been given the chance to wish for anything in the world but instead of asking for wealth or power or beauty or fame the way that anybody else might do, she decides to keep her wish, to save it for her child. To Mollie, this seemed to be such an impossible act of generosity, an all-but-unbearable manifestation of true maternal love. She was convinced that her own mother would never have done anything like that—she would have asked for a million dollars, probably, or a new house, or a dishwasher, or a car. But this woman, Alice Bell, she wanted nothing for herself, and our Mollie Mifflin had fallen flat in love with her for that.

Chapter Six

Mollie found John Steele's office on the second floor, there in the old wing of Stanley Hall. At the far end of a long hallway, tucked in next to the stairs, it wasn't the best office—that was the one that belonged to Fabricunt—but it wasn't the worst one either. Mr. Steele's was only a temporary appointment, and so he didn't get a real sign on his door—instead his name had been hand-written in careful calligraphy rendered in purple ink with silver stick-em stars scattered around it for decoration on a rectangle of poster board that had been tacked by four corners to the middle of the door. The work of some lovesick co-ed, no doubt, who had read his book and wept.

"John Steele" it said, plain and simple. He was not a professor; he was just a writer, after all—not even a novelist, just another guy who'd had a crummy childhood like everybody else, except that he had made a book out of his while the rest of us are left to wallow in our own bad dreams. By contrast, a permanent bronze plaque had been mounted on a nearby wall, with Deek's name on it, evidence that this had been his office once, too, all those years ago, when he first came to Brevity with Emily. That one, too, read simply: Deacon Bensenhaver Molene. What else was there to say?

Mollie knocked, stood back, and listened. Waited, knocked again, a hopeful patter of knuckles on wood, but obviously, Mr. Steele was not in. She figured it was likely that he kept his office hours in the afternoon, like everybody else in the writing program—it was well known that the classes and workshops were usually held late in the day because the writers who came to teach preferred to do their own work first thing in the morning. Get it over with, early on, leave them free to teach and talk and criticize everybody else's stuff all afternoon and, sometimes, on into the night. Or maybe they just needed the mornings after to sleep off the effects of the night before.

The building itself was quiet and clean. Sparkling black and white tiled floor. Butter yellow walls, giving it a warm, optimistic air. There was the requisite bulletin board papered with layers of announcements—room available, typing services, housekeeper wanted. Plus, the usual sardonic "New Yorker" cartoons, submission calls to obscure literary magazines, offers for scholarship applications, and an invitation to an "Open Mike" night in the Student Lounge on Wednesday at seven-thirty. Below this sat the bins for the pages to be read and workshopped in the classes, with each leader's name labeling each bin. Mollie picked up one of the stories and gave it a glance—something about gang rape in a swimming pool at a birthday party, full of exclamation points, footnotes, and bold face type. Freshman stuff.

Down the hall, a door was standing partly open, and when she positioned herself just so at the drinking fountain, Mollie could see some of the class that was in progress inside. Rows of free-standing desks, students sprawled in their seats, looking sleepy, and at the front of the room, Mouse Wendler was standing at the board. She was scrawling something, and the chalk squeaked before she turned around, waiting for a response. They seemed to be studying grammar, conjugating verbs. Working on the past perfect tense, it looked like. I had loved, you had loved, he had loved, and so on.

Mollie figured that all she could do was wait for Mr. Steele to come in because she didn't know how else to find him—at that time she didn't even know where he and Sarah lived—and so she sat against the wall beside his office door, huddled on the cold floor with her chin on her knees and her arms wrapped around her legs, hugging herself tight. She was wearing her own jeans and a T-shirt by then, too, one that she'd bought at a swap meet, with a goofy red happy face on the front, and sneakers as well—practical clothes, just in case she had to do any running or jumping. Or breaking in.

Plato was downstairs, leashed to the bike rack outside the building, sitting on his haunches, ears perked, waiting hopefully for Emily or Deek, especially Deek, to show up so life could go back to being the way that it was before.

A clacking on the stairs signaled the arrival of Joyce Blanding—she was using a white cane to find the way to her own office down the hall. Mollie sat perfectly still with the hope that, being blind, The Widow wouldn't know she was there. Bre'r Fox, laying low again.

Not that Mollie had any reason to hide, she just didn't want to have to do any more explaining to anybody, not if she could help it. What had happened, why she was there, what she was going to do next. She'd already told so many lies in the past couple of days that she was starting to lose track of her own confabulations, and she was beginning to feel the web of her deceit starting to close in to trap and eat her up alive.

The Widow clacked past, stopped at her own office door, pulled a big ring of keys out of her purse, then turned and listened. She seemed to be looking right at Mollie, so directly that for a second, she was thinking that behind the milk scum on her eyeballs the Widow was actually faking it, that she was not really blind after all. But the Widow didn't say anything or give any other indication that she was in any way aware that Mollie was there and was watching her. She finally just turned the key and went inside and closed her door behind her, so maybe Mollie was wrong. The Widow's own nameplate was black plastic with white letters and a secret-seeming code of Braille dots and dashes embossed underneath it, just in case she ever needed to read it for herself.

Mollie let her chin rest on her knees again, and she closed her eyes and dozed. She was thinking about all the lies she'd told in her life and about all that had happened in the last few months, how her world had become so completely changed ever since it had commenced on that fateful night of her graduation, when she found her mother sitting on the front porch and all her stuff spread out all over the yard for everybody to see. And so then there it was, that old familiar ache of self-pity welling up inside her again, now. She was aware of it, coming on so strong that if she'd been alone and unobserved she would have had to call on Horace to slap herself around a bit and bring her back to her senses again. As it was, she was saved from this by the bell—though it wasn't really a bell, just a creaking open of the doors and a shuffling of desks and books and papers and students filing out into the hall, making enough noise to distract Mollie from herself again, for which she was deeply grateful.

Trooping past her, jostling each other along the way, here were these young people of privilege in this posh private college where they were learning to read good books and add up numbers and understand something about the origin of the universe and the historical past that had brought them there and made them what they were, so that when they were done they could step into the future by taking charge of the family business and still have something interesting to talk about at the cocktail parties and the barbecues back home.

Mollie stood up and joined them, thinking just for that moment that she might even be about to become one of them herself, because looking at them, really, who could tell the difference? But before she could lose herself completely in the entitlement of their boisterous crowd, she was jerked back to her true place again by a hand on her arm.

"Mollie!" And that was just exactly what she did not want just then, laying low as she was. She did not want to be noticed, to be recognized, to be singled out as herself. But, "What are you doing here?" She turned to see Mouse Wendler, her face a friendly crumple of concern. "I thought—" Mouse began, but Mollie interrupted her.

"You teach here?" she asked, like that was a big surprise.

Mouse explained about how she was a TA, exploited by the college, monitoring the extra credit study groups that the real professors didn't want to bother with in exchange for a break in the cost of her tuition. Composition and rhetoric. Grammar, punctuation, spelling, and vocabulary. She stopped and studied Mollie. "Hey, but are you okay?" she asked.

"Sure," Mollie replied, shrugging herself away. She wasn't trying to be rude but, "I'm fine."

They were eye to eye, and maybe Mouse saw the hostility in Mollie's face because she let go of her arm and backed off a bit. "How are the Molenes?"

Mollie sighed, dramatically. "They're in the hospital. I don't know. I think it's bad."

Mouse frowned. "Oh," she said. "I'm sorry." She

looked at her watch. It was a pink plastic Hello Kitty design, very camp. "Listen, I have to run. But if there's anything I can do…" Already she had turned away and was skittering down the stairs. "Call me!" And she was gone.

Mollie looked at the Widow's door. Stepped closer, put out a fist and tap-tap-tapped. She listened, then tapped again. Nothing. She took hold of the knob, turned it, peered in. "Excuse me?"

A stirring, jangle of silver, a voice, soft, "What is it?"

Mollie stepped inside. The office was dim, lit by the light that filtered through the venetian blinds at the windows. The Widow was curled like a spider on a chair. "Who's there?"

"Excuse me, Professor Blanding?"

Her face was pale, glowing. A candle burned, casting yellow light flickering and shining in the jewelry she wore.

Mollie pulled the door closed behind her. "My name is Mollie. I work for the Molenes?"

The Widow smiled. "Oh yes. You're the girl."

Mollie nodded, then realized that, of course, the Widow couldn't see her. "That's right," she said. "I suppose you've heard…"

"Yes." She shook her head. "It sounds bad."

Mollie had no choice then; the old survival machine kicked into gear all on its own, and she began to lie as fiercely as ever. She didn't know what else to do. She said that Emily and Deek were just fine. It was no big deal. They'd be coming home, soon. Later Joyce Blanding would remember this and think that Mollie was in denial about death, and she'd want to help her through that, but by then it would be too late.

What if the candle fell over and set this place on fire? Was it safe, a blind woman with a candle burning? Mollie resisted the temptation to lean over and blow it out. (More than 15,000 residential fires are caused each year by the careless or inappropriate use of candles. Bedroom 38%, living/family room/den 15%, bathroom 14%, kitchen 8%.)

"I'm so sorry to bother you, Professor Blanding," Mollie went on.

She waved her hand, impatiently. "Please, call me Joyce. I'm a poet, not a professor."

"Of course. Joyce. I'm sorry to bother you, but, um… I was looking for Mr. Steele?"

"But this is my office, not his." She said this tentatively, as if she wasn't really sure whether it was true.

"Yes, I know. But I thought maybe…" What? What did she think? "I thought you might know how I might find him." Why would she know? She's blind!

Joyce pulled herself up from the sofa and stood next to her desk, then leaned over and blew out the candle, throwing the room into further darkness. "I believe he has a workshop later this afternoon," she said.

"I know," Mollie replied, calm as cake, and then she felt compelled to say more, and like she was some kind of girl-style Pinocchio, the lies just started pouring forth, one after the other, until there seemed to be no hope of stopping them anymore. "I'm in it," she said, "but after all that's happened, well, I've been so busy, what with keeping track of everything and looking for a new job and all that, so I'm not going to be able to be there. I wanted to tell him that, in person, let him know, so he doesn't think I'm skipping out on my first day or something." She paused. The Widow seemed to be buying it, so Mollie plunged on and got right to the point: "Do you know where he lives, by any chance?"

One step too far, maybe, and this seemed to trouble the Widow. She frowned, looked at Mollie with a quizzical expression on her face. "Why?"

Backtracking, trying to come up with something reasonable. "I don't know. I guess I thought I might go over to his house, see if I could maybe talk to him, you know. Tell him about what happened? That's all."

The Widow cocked her head the other way. "I'm sure he's probably heard about what happened."

Mollie nodded. Sure, sure. And then, "If I flunk out of here, my mother will never forgive me… " Where had that come from? But she had the right look on her face and tears were stinging her eyes again—why did she always have to resort to that? Because it worked?—though these dramatics were wasted on the Widow, who wasn't able to see them. Still, she must have sensed how upset Mollie was.

"How about we call him, would that help?" She found the roster, and Mollie could see the address on it. 112 Bridge Street. The Widow handed her the phone—the numbers were in Braille. Mollie felt her face go red. Seriously, sometimes she had no control at all. She hung up the phone.

"No, that's okay," she said. "You're right. And he probably won't care anyway. I just get over-dramatic sometimes. It's a flaw. I've always been that way. Drama queen, my sister calls me. Says I should go into show business. But my mother says it's going to make me a great writer someday." Blah blah blah blah, and then, pause, she took a breath, let the explanation sink in. "So, I can talk to him later all right I guess. I don't want to bother him at home, when he's working. That wouldn't be right, I know that. He's probably writing or something. I wouldn't want to interrupt the artistic process in any way with my own small personal concerns." Mollie was talking faster now, as she backed away, thanking the Widow, gushing until she got to the doorway, where she said goodbye and thank you again, one more time before she pulled the door closed after her, leaving the widow in the dark, and clambered down the stairs to the street.

Once she had the address, Mollie had no trouble finding the Steeles' house—Brevity is indeed brief.

She was careful in her approach, because the last thing she wanted to do was to come on too strong and fast and risk scaring anybody off. She had Plato on the leash, and she was following Postscript's advice this time, acting like she knew what she was doing. She walked right up onto the porch, knocked softly at the door, pressed a thumb to the bell, listened to its muffled chime. Footsteps, and then she was gratified to see the face of Sarah Steele peering through the glass almost exactly the same way that Emily had on that first night of Mollie's appearance in Brevity. She took this to be a good sign that she was on the right track, all right, and so gave Sarah her brightest smile, with a little four-fingered tiddly wave to go with it. Friendly-like. Girlish.

Piping up, hopefully: "Excuse me, Mrs. Steele?" Keeping up the front for now, keeping up appearances until they were safely inside and could talk more freely, privately, between themselves. Mollie was still willing to keep the secret then, if that was what they thought they wanted, still prepared to play along, hadn't really thought it all the way through to a conclusion yet, hadn't yet considered the consequences of what they'd done, or measured up the cost.

Plato sat obediently by her side, an accomplice, partner in crime, and he was panting and unconcerned, as though he knew exactly what was going on and this was all just a small part of someone else's larger plan.

Sarah opened the door then, and Plato whined—he seemed to be excited to see her, and Mollie had to hold him back or he'd have been jumping up and slobbering all over Sarah's face. This, the second bit of confirmation that Mollie was barking up the right alley. (Or whatever.) Anyway, Plato seemed to know Sarah, all right.

For her part, Sarah looked appropriately annoyed, and Mollie could guess at what she was about to say: "No solicitations, sorry. We already gave. Thanks anyway." She had to admire the authenticity of Sarah's reaction to the sight of her so far. She had fallen into her part in this little scene just like she was born to it. Her bright blond hair was clamped back by a fat black barrette, loose hairs wisped prettily around her face—she looked so real. Mollie might have faltered then, might have fallen for the disguise herself, that's how perfect it was. Even though she knew better, and she was not expecting Sarah to break into irony. Not yet.

She was holding a paintbrush in her hand, convincing prop. And she was wearing an apron that said, "Kiss the cook!" with paint spattered across the front, Jackson Pollock-style. Underneath, a baby-doll T-shirt and sweatpants that she'd hacked off above the knee. Later she would be telling Mollie, still keeping up the front: "Gosh, I never knew Iowa was this hot! And in September!" Turquoise rubber flip-flops with a flower on the toe. A rose, of course. What else?

Mollie's grin was manic. "Hi!"

Sarah seemed puzzled. "Can I help you?"

For herself, Mollie could not stop smiling. Her guard was down, and she'd gone all goofy, giggly like Postscript, when he was high.

Sarah's own bewilderment was charming. She was peering at Mollie more closely. "Do I know you?"

Mollie just smiled away, waiting for Sarah to give

in and drop the façade. A wink—she couldn't resist. Then slyly: "Yes, ma'am, I think you do."

Sarah stared at her for a moment, as if Mollie were an alien or something, a freak of a kind that she had never seen before in her life, and it was clear that she was not sure how to handle the situation, exactly. Her face flushed pink with embarrassment and confusion, like she could not figure out if this was a joke and she had missed something, and she deserved an Academy Award for that performance, seriously.

Mollie stayed put, all patience; she could wait, however long it was going to take—she used to beat her sister at staring contests (which Janet would be the one to initiate, by the way) all the time. And then, finally there it was, a spark of recognition. Aha! Sarah was nodding now, and smiling. Waving her paintbrush at Mollie gaily, saying, "Oh yes, of course! I saw you at the Dr. Phillips' party, didn't I?"

So that was how it was going to be. Okay, Mollie could play along for a while, if that was what Sarah was into. And so she nodded with enthusiasm. "Yes, that was me! Mollie Mifflin. I work for the Molenes. Or at least I did. Until…"

Sarah frowned. Winced, clucked, and shook her head. Pierced Mollie's heart straight through with a motherly look of compassion and concern that seemed altogether genuine. "I'm so sorry," she said. And then: "Come in, Mollie. Please."

So she left Plato out on the porch and followed Sarah into the house. He seemed happy to stay out there, as if he knew that this was where he really belonged. He lay down on the mat and set his chin on his paws again.

Inside, it looked like the Steeles were still in the process of moving in, and the house was a big mess of boxes, not yet unpacked, or opened and rummaged through. Kitchen utensils had been left in the living room. Dishes still wrapped in newspaper were piled up on the sofa. Clearly, this Sarah Steele could have used some help, and Mollie was, once again, just the girl for that.

Sarah's paints and papers had been set up in the dining room, on the long walnut table, and everything looked like it was in pretty good order there at least. Jars bristling with brushes. Tubes of paints, squashed and squeezed. Plastic palettes, color-daubed. Postcards. Books. Photographs. A CD player murmuring some whispery new-age melodies—flutes and violins.

Sarah laughed. "The house is a big mess, I know," she said. She waved a hand, indicating the unpacked boxes on the floor. Tried to wipe her hair out of her face, putting a smear of paint across her temple instead. "I had a deadline, and I missed it. My publisher is *not* happy. He's been calling me all day." Even at its most pained, that smile of hers did dazzle. "But I don't seem to be able to do anything right," she told Mollie, and the smile faded, gone under a cloud. "Maybe I've lost the knack."

Her pretty face was pink now, with embarrassment, it seemed. Or frustration, maybe. And it did look like she'd been having a tough enough time of it, going by the wads of crumpled paper all over the floor. On the table there was a small, tentative drawing of a mouth blowing out candles. With the neatly printed invitation to: "Make a wish! It's your birthday!" Not bad, considering.

She brushed her hands on her thighs, pressing the apron flat across her front. She tilted her head and squinted at the drawing, her own mouth pursed, brow creased, and then she seemed to shake herself out of it. "I'm sorry," she said, turning to Mollie. "Would you like something? I've just made a fresh pot of coffee. Are you hungry?"

Mollie shrugged and stammered, as usual. "Sure, thanks. That would be awesome." Like she was a stray cat being brought in. Or an orphan. Or maybe just a distraction. Maybe Sarah was glad to be able to turn away from the work for a while because obviously it had not been going well at all. She'd either lost the knack, all right, or she'd never had it in the first place.

Mollie followed her into the kitchen—which was even more of a mess than the rest of the house, with cupboard doors open and dirty dishes in the sink. Sarah poured coffee and spilled some cookies out onto a plate. She cleared the little breakfast table under the window, and they sat across from each other. Sarah was watching Mollie, who sipped her coffee (weak). Nibbled a cookie (stale). Let Sarah make the first move.

"So," she said. Outside the window, a cat was sitting on a fencepost, tail twitching.

Even though it was obvious that Sarah couldn't think of a thing to say to Mollie, she still seemed to be glad for the interruption and maybe for the company, too. The ceiling creaked as someone walked across the floor upstairs, and they both glanced up—John, most likely, pretending to be normal, acting like he was working, too.

Sarah said something, but Mollie didn't quite catch it. Something like, "What a day." Or, "I'm this way." Or, "It's okay." And then she flashed that smile of hers again, and Mollie got the impression that she was trying to reassure her—let her know, without saying so outright, that everything was going to be all right. They lapsed into silence again, and it was uncomfortable now, as Sarah fiddled with the fringe on her placemat. Mollie didn't know what to say to her; she didn't know where to begin. There seemed to be so much to talk about and at the same time, nothing. Finally Sarah cleared her throat, then stood and brushed her hands through her hair. "Well, then..."

What could Mollie say? Finally she just came out with it. "I know who you are."

"I beg your pardon?"

Mollie smiled. Waved her hands around. "The goblets, the brandy. All that."

Still Sarah seemed baffled. And Mollie thought, Okay, I can play along then, if that's what she wants. She realized that, of course, they would want to keep it a secret. Because first of all, who would believe them? And second of all... Well, that was enough—who would believe them?

And so: On Sarah's blank look, Mollie grins, spreads her arms, as if to say, It worked! Because, she's the angel, right? And it had all been her idea in the first place. Sarah is still playing the puzzled innocent though, so, "It's okay," Mollie says. "I won't tell anybody." And then goes on, full steam: "I think it's amazing. Very cool. A full-blown, true-to-life, as-real--as-it-gets miracle!"

It was just then that John came into the room, coffee mug in hand. Also: brown corduroys, big cardigan sweater, rumpled hair, tortoise-shell specs: he was the picture of a professor. Or a writer. This was, of course, a role he knew exactly how to play. He was polite, maybe a little defensive, in a careful sort of way. Like he was just waiting to see how the scene was going to go before he decided whether he'd step in, push his weight around, rescue his wife from what looked to be an uncomfortable situation. He leaned over and kissed her—sweet matrimonial peck on the cheekbone, a proprietary gesture, Mollie thought, meant to make it clear who belonged to whom. "What's a miracle?" he asked.

Sarah's face was still blank. She shrugged. "I have no idea," she said.

John was looking at Mollie expectantly. She introduced herself. He shook her hand. "Pleased to meet you." Very cordial. Very polite. Even as he seemed to be winking at her. The ball was in her court, and he was waiting for her to go on.

It was like the three of them had this big secret between them, an elephant in the room that they were all squeezing their way around. And for Mollie's part, she couldn't see how there was really anything for her to do but just play along with it and act like she didn't know that the elephant was there. She could see why they wouldn't want to give their secret away, and that was okay with her, for now. She hadn't considered the real consequences yet, either.

John was acting like he was trying to figure out who she was, much less what she was doing there. He gave her a good once-over, taking in the hair, the piercings, the tattoo. "You're a student?"

Good guess, but... "Well, no. Not yet, that is. Except for a class I took last summer with the Goat..." Smile, as she waited for the response to this, the little joke that she and Deek had had going between them about Dr. Phillips, and she was expecting him to get it then, but if he did, he gave no sign. So she said Dr. Phillips' real name and John didn't even smile, he just nodded, like he was thinking about it, and the silence got all thick and uncomfortable again as he poured some coffee into a metal travel mug.

"Your wife here," Mollie said, "she's the real writer in the family, right?" Wink wink. She thought she caught a quick look exchanged between them that might have meant: "What are we going to do about this?" Or it could have been: "What the hell is she talking about?" She wished she had Postscript there to help her out. She really was no good at reading minds, and he was always excellent at cutting through the bullshit to get directly to the point.

John screwed the top down on the mug, giving it all his attention, then turned to Mollie. "Will you be applying?"

The twinkle in his eye made her blush. It was one thing when Deek looked at her like that, lecherous old fart, but when John did it... no liver lips, no yellow teeth. John was young and handsome, in his way. ("Boy crazy!" her mother had yelled at Janet. Mollie cowering in her room.) She cleared her throat, fiddled with one of the studs in her right ear. She told him she was only an undergraduate, not even that, since she had finished high school just last spring and hadn't enrolled in college yet. It was awkward. He was embarrassed, and she was embarrassed, and Sarah was looking at the two of them as if she'd discovered they've been having an affair or something.

Mollie threw it back at him. "You must be looking forward to teaching here."

He didn't respond. Just looked at her as if he were waiting for her to say more. He didn't look at Sarah, either. Mollie felt like he was challenging her. His brother the psycho killer, she thought, and now he sort of had that look, too. What if they'd got switched somehow. She was following this train of thought when she reminded herself that no, this wasn't John Steele, anyway. This was Deek Molene, and he was playing with her. Deliberately trying to scare her. To put her off the track. "Lots of beautiful young women, I mean." She winked at Sarah.

They both stared at her. "Well," John said finally, picking up his briefcase and checking his watch. She noticed that the twinkle was gone from his eyes. He was done playing, it seemed. "It's been very nice to meet you..." He was looking at her like he'd forgotten her name. She told him again and he nodded, but didn't say it. He turned to his wife and said he'd see her tonight and have a nice day and so on and so forth, like a 1950's TV sitcom or something. He was playing it to the hilt, all right. He kissed Sarah on the forehead this time and then headed for the front door, and Mollie was looking at her, wondering why she didn't explain about who she was, her connection to the Molenes, to her! To John! Hey, Mollie was thinking, hasn't this gone far enough? Come on now, let's get real!

Plato was still out there on the porch, and he was on his feet and barking at John, who stood back like he'd never seen a German shepherd before, or at least not this one, and at that point Mollie was starting to get pissed off.

"What's this?" John said, like he didn't know.

She heard herself apologize, like she didn't know either. "Sorry," she said. "That's just my dog." And then corrected that with, "Well, he's not exactly my dog. He belongs to the Molenes?" She made this sound like a question, a loaded one: like, You know them, right? You *are* them, right? But before John could answer, Sarah piped up; she'd found her voice ,and she was finally telling him who Mollie was—the Molenes' housekeeper, is how she put it. She didn't say angel, she didn't say caretaker, she didn't say nurse. She didn't say "our own good girl." No, she called Mollie the housekeeper. Like she was just the cleaning lady or something.

John's response? "Oh, good," he said, looking at her again now, as if he were reassessing his first impression. "We could use a little help around here."

And then he was gone, leaving Sarah and Mollie to stand there on the porch with Plato, watching him as he headed down the street toward campus.

John waved without looking back at them; he just raised his hand up over his head and tootle-ooed his fingers before he rounded the corner and was gone.

Mollie heard Sarah sigh. She saw her frown. She didn't know yet that Sarah was pregnant, and if she was really Emily Molene, then probably neither did she. Mollie might have confronted her then. She might have said, "Okay, Emily, enough's enough." Hands on her hips and that same frank look that her mother would get when she caught her at her old tricks—sneaking out of the house, sneaking back into the house, smoking a cigarette in her room, hiding stolen merchandise under her bed—asking her, "Who do you think you're kidding, Mollie?" Telling her, "You're only hurting yourself."

But the phone rang just then, and Sarah didn't even glance at Mollie; she just turned on her heel and went back inside. Like she wasn't ready to deal with this girl and her questions and her knowledge and her accusations, not just yet.

She left the door open, though, and Mollie took that to be her cue, and she acted on it. She waited until she was sure that Sarah had picked up the phone and was talking to someone, and then she let herself in and went to work at cleaning up the kitchen. Just like old times.

She thought: If this is going to be the game, then count me in.

Mollie had no doubts that she was right about what had happened. It was obvious to her that the comparatively youthful bodies of Sarah and John Steele had been taken over by the older souls of Emily and Deek Molene. That had been their wish—to be young again—and this was how it was to be fulfilled. Hard as it may have been to believe, it all made perfect sense, and it was not even that hard to imagine. In fact, she was pretty sure she could pinpoint the exact moment when it had happened because hadn't she seen it for herself? At the Grotto, when everybody was dancing. John, looking like he'd been struck by lightning, and Sarah vague, lost, as if she didn't know where she was. Or who.

Deek and Emily would have been at home, in the study. They would have already made their wish. The night dark, rain drizzling against the windowpanes. A full moon in the sky, scumbled by shredded clouds.

Emily standing by her chair, eyes closed and fingers crossed, and Deek, still doubtful, reaching for her. A low humming sound filling their ears and then growing beyond them, stronger, fuller, the murmur of a million voices buzzing, a deep deafening thunderous roar. Emily's eyes popping open. "Oh..." Dizzy, rising, floating, swimming. She swoons and slumps to the floor.

"Emily?" A lightning flash seems to hit right there in the room, blinding him. He grabs his head, the immediate crack of thunder feels like it's exploded inside his own body, it's that close. He staggers, falls, pulling the table down with a crash. The goblets roll, spilled brandy seeps into the carpet.

Deek and Emily are on the floor. Blood trickles from Deek's nose. Emily's breath rattles in her chest.

While at the Grotto, out on the dance floor, John Steele is feeling woozy. He knows he's had too much to drink. He looks around the room to see people moving, a blur of color—at the tables and in the booths they're eating, drinking, laughing, talking. Sound seems magnified. He sees Sarah across the room and suddenly, inexplicably, he longs for her. He takes a step toward her, thinks to call out her name, but he can't see clearly, everything looks smoky, sparkly, and the music has changed, becoming louder; it's a deeper buzz in his ears that seems to be coming from inside him now. He closes his eyes. Wavers. Someone is touching him, "Professor Steele, are you okay?" He blinks, confused. A girl is handing him a napkin. He wipes at his face and sees that his nose is bleeding. He squeezes his nostrils between forefinger and thumb and holds his other hand out in front of him, turning it, studying it. He touches his own face with his fingertips and grins. "Ha!" he says. He's laughing like crazy. Jumping up and down, or maybe he's dancing because the music has changed, and now they're playing a fast song.

He looks around, searching frantically through the crowd. Where the hell is she?

She's in Dr. Phillips' arms, that's where. She's been watching John over Dr. Phillips' shoulder, keeping an eye on his drinking. She's seen the blood on his face, and she's started to pull away, but a darkness has seeped over her now, too, like a drawn shade. She stumbles into Dr. Phillips; he looks up at her, surprised. "Sarah?" His hand is on her arm, but she jumps back at his touch. Looks at him, puzzled. How did she get here? With this man? "Oh my, I..."

She starts to faint, but now here is John Steele, he's caught her in his arms. He holds her. Dr. Phillips backs away.

Sarah looks down at herself and then at John again. "Deek?" she asks. His hands are moving over her body; he gently runs his fingers over the contour of her face, her neck, her shoulders, her breasts. She steps back. "Oh!"

"Emily!" He pulls her to him again, takes her in his arms. She stiffens and tries to avert her face, but she can't. She is looking into John Steele's eyes and seeing there Deek Molene's wisdom, his humor, his love, and she realizes that he is seeing her in Sarah, too.

How could they know for sure that it was real? The light that each one saw there in the other's eyes? The recognition of an eternal love. These two were soul mates, after all.

They kiss under the confetti light of the mirror ball, and the others on the dance floor stand back to admire.

While moonlight shines through the curtains in the study of the Molenes' house and falls on the body of Emily on the floor. She begins to stir. She sits up and looks around, confused, where is she? How did she get here? She can see an old man lying on his back near her, and only after a moment of gazing at him does she realize that it is Deek Molene. She crawls over to him, and when she reaches out to touch him, that's when she notices her own hand. The wrinkles. The large veins. The liver spots. She looks down at the rest her body now, and when she sees what she's become she scrambles to her feet, whimpering, brushing at herself, trying to shrug herself out of her own decrepit flesh.

Hard to imagine Sarah's horror. It must have totally blown the poor girl's mind.

We know what people are going to want to say when they read this, our explanation for everything that happened to Mollie, to the Molenes, to the Steeles. There will be some who will conclude that Mollie is crazy, or at least that she has made this whole thing up with such conviction that eventually she's even come to believe it herself, which isn't exactly the same as being crazy, but it's close. To get attention or embarrass her family or maybe just to suit her own fantasy. Mollie and those Columbine boys or Brenda Spencer ("I don't like Mondays") or Mark David Chapman himself. All those looney-tunes out there on the streets hearing voices and seeing visions, all those nobodies going after somebodies just to make a name for themselves, setting out to commit the worst kinds of self-aggrandizing crimes that are just flagrant enough to get them on TV and in the newspapers and the history books so they start to think they've maybe found a way to live forever.

But our Mollie Mifflin is not one of those. She is not glory-mongering, and she is not crazy, and she is not a murderer, either. Mollie is just trying to do what's right, that's all, because the voices she hears and the visions she sees? They are real.

Sure, it's hard to believe. Nobody these days thinks that this sort of thing can happen anymore. Not in real life. How could it? Impossible! "Get real," Mollie's sister tells her. "Time to grow up, Mollie," her mother says. "There is a rational explanation for everything," her father insists. The laws of science do not bend. And numbers do not lie. What you see is what you get. The world is all there is.

Right, and the earth is flat, and you can't send a rocket to the moon, and there was no second gunman on the grassy knoll. No hidden bombs in the Twin Towers, no New World Order, no Illuminati, no Bilderberg Group, no UFOs, no Peak Oil or Montauk or HAARP. But listen to this: our friend Postscript? He got out. Genius that he was, he Houdini-ed his way free of the Juvie Jail. He slipped away when nobody was looking, and then that little fucker figured out a way to get even and at the same time set himself finally and forever free.

Mollie's own dad, Mr. Skeptical himself, he was the one who told her that someday people will be able to live forever, and when that happens, he'll be out of a job because then there won't be any need for life insurance or actuaries such as himself anymore. He was talking about his own dad, Mollie's big fat grump of a grandfather, and the hip replacements that he'd had, one after the other, a few years ago, and then he was as good as new. Almost. Mr. Mifflin goes: "If they can make artificial bones and limbs and hearts, why not artificial kidneys and livers, too? Why not artificial blood and guts and skin? Why not artificial whole bodies?" Why not? "It's only a matter of time," he said.

And once they've got that all figured out, then all they have to do is start programming computers to think and act just like people. You pay somebody to make a computer that can behave as if it's you—saying all the things that you would say in just the exact same way that you would say them, doing the things that you would do, acting the way that you would act, with just enough discrepancy to make it totally believable, and then when your brain dies of old age, as it will—there just is not any getting around that—then they just put that computer inside the new empty head of your already artificial body, and there you are, the same as you ever were. Maybe even more so. So much so, in fact, that nobody, not even your own children, can tell the difference anymore.

Nobody but you, that is. Because, of course, you're dead. Whatever that means. Aren't you? What is it to be yourself, anyway? Are you what you think you are on the inside, or are you what people see of you from the outside? If everybody believed that John and Sarah Steele were really John and Sarah Steele, then that must have been who they were, right? Even when Mollie, for one, knew for a fact that they were really Deek and Emily Molene?

Postscript grabs his head and pulls at his hair. He lisps: "Mollie! That ith tho fucked up!"

No shit, Postscript. No shit.

CHAPTER SEVEN

http://www.badideas.com/pgpgbmb.html
How to Build a Plastic Golf Ball Bomb
by Donald J. Walters

IMPORTANT NOTICE TO ALL CONCERNED: Certain text files and messages contained on this website deal with activities and devices which would be in violation of various Federal, State, and Local laws if actually carried out as instructed. The webmasters of this site do not advocate the breaking of any law. Our text files and message boards are for informational purposes only. We recommend that you contact your local law enforcement officials before undertaking any project based upon any information obtained from this or any other website. We do not guarantee that any of the information contained on this system is correct, workable, or factual. We are not responsible for, nor do we assume any liability for, damages resulting from the use of any information on this site.

MATERIALS:
Hot glue or duct tape
Plastic Ping-Pong ball
A razor blade or sharp knife
Light-anywhere matches
Sandpaper
Scissors
Pyrodex (optional)

PROCEDURE:

Cut up enough match-heads to fill the Ping--Pong ball 3/4 of the way.

Cut a strip of sandpaper.

Cut a hole in the top of the Ping-Pong ball.

Stick both the matches and the sandpaper into the Ping-Pong ball hole.

Put hot glue or duct tape over the hole in the ball. [Tip: Make sure no air can escape, or else this won't work.]

Go outside and start throwing the ball hard against the ground (pavement, not grass). It may not work the first few tries, but if you keep chucking it, it will eventually explode.

This is probably the easiest explosive to make, and these materials will be around your house, so you probably won't even have to go out and buy anything. But if you want to make a real big bang, you can add some Pyrodex to the mix. Cover your ears!

[IMPORTANT NOTE: Throw the ball away from your body because it could explode and really fuck you up.]

Well, unless that's the whole point. In which case, spring for an extra roll of duct tape, take several Ping-Pong balls—as many as forty of them or even more for a greater effect— and string them together with the tape. Then, wrap the whole thing around your neck, several times, like some kind of a freaky, funky necklace. You could paint the Ping-Pong balls different colors, too, if that seems more glamorous to you. Fingernail polish works well. When the time is right, use a Bic lighter to ignite the first ball and… Boom! Boom! Boom!

Baby, you're on fire!

Would you rather die young? Kerpow, or natural causes? Is it better to burn out than to fade away? Better to go out with a bang than with a whimper? Out of the blue and into the black?

If you could live forever, would you do it?

Who was going to be the one who would blame Deek and Emily Molene for what they did? Who would, in their position, have had the strength to do anything else than what they did? Just try to imagine what it must have been like for them, to have those bodies, to be able to start all over again, practically brand new. Youth, isn't that what everybody wants? To live forever, forever young? To start all over, square one?

This was what Postscript's father did, isn't it? Married again after his first wife died, and then the second one was pregnant, and he was a dad again and could have a whole new life for himself, a second chance, and he didn't even have to die to do it. He would raise those kids, do for them what he had never done for his first family because now he knew better; he was older and he was smarter and it was easier, somehow. Never mind where that left little Paul Solomon, out on his own and all alone, tied to a pole in the back yard, like a dog.

Who can blame Deek and Emily for not wanting to take back their wish and give their own second chances up? Who can blame them for trying to hide the truth of what they had done? Not us. Nope, when it comes to the Molenes, we are an encyclopedia of understanding, a fountain of compassion, a well of imaginative empathy, as deep as the deepest sea. But that doesn't mean that what they did was right. And it doesn't mean, either, that Mollie didn't feel compelled to do something about it. It doesn't mean that she didn't intend to do everything in her power to set things straight again and get those folks put back into their own bodies, where they belonged.

Because, what about Sarah Steele?

When Sarah got off the phone after John walked off to work that day, when she came back into the kitchen again, there Mollie was at the sink, up to her elbows in soapsuds, grinning like a maniac over her shoulder at her, trying to smile her way back into Emily's good graces.

"You're still here," Sarah said. There were tears in her eyes, and she was wiping at them with the back of her wrist, composing herself. Her publisher must have drubbed her pretty good.

And there Mollie was, too, nodding, grinning, slopping a sponge over a pile of dirty plates. "Yup, still here, that's exactly what I am. You and me both."

Maybe Mollie was thinking now that they were alone, Emily would be able to let her guard down and give a glimpse of her old self as Mollie imagined it, encased like a nut inside the firm fresh shell of Sarah Steele's perfect flesh. She was upset, that much was clear. But, Mollie reasoned, if anybody could help her now, she was the one for the job. Because she was the only other person in the world who understood what had happened, she was the only other person who could sympathize, the only other person who knew Emily and could talk to her about who she really was. Mollie took her hands out of the water, dried them on a towel, ready now for her to come clean. She turned to face her. "Emily?"

Sarah was blowing her nose, and maybe she didn't hear Mollie say the name. Mollie moved closer to her, thinking now was the time for her to put an arm around her, to tell her it was all right, that everything was going to be okay, she was here, she'd take care of her, she'd help her sort things out, just as she'd always done. She was her angel, wasn't she?

But Sarah was already getting a grip on herself, she was pushing Mollie away and shaking her head, lifting her chin, squaring her shoulders. Deep breath, and she was apologizing, "Oh God, I'm so sorry, this is so embarrassing, I don't know what's wrong with me, it was a bad morning." And then, "I guess I'm just not myself today."

No, she wasn't, was she?, but that was not something Mollie said out loud. She didn't want to scare Emily off, not now, not when she was finally starting to break down. And so instead she offered to help her out, that's all. Harmless enough. All she said was, "At least let's get you unpacked. You'll feel better when you've made yourself at home here."

Sarah thought about this for a minute. "I'll have to pay you," she said, and Mollie told her that was just fine with her. Sarah asked: "How much did you charge the Molenes for your services?" Eyes wide. As if she didn't know. Mollie reminded her, and she said that sounded fair. Then she went upstairs to lie down.

Maybe it would be cooler if we could say that Mollie found a home pregnancy test in the trash with a big fat plus sign on it. Or that she found Sarah's diary while she was going through her things. Or that Sarah took Mollie aside and told her about it herself, girl to girl, best friend, confidante-style. Or even that Mollie was able to read Sarah's mind. But that's not how it happened. It wasn't a discovery Mollie had to make anyway because she could tell what was up just by looking at her. She'd already seen it in her sister's face twice, that look. Sarah didn't have to say a word. It was totally obvious that she was pregnant, and she must have known it, too. So, no wonder that Emily, who had been childless in her first life, was freaking out about it now. Don't forget what happened to the man who suddenly *got everything he ever wanted.*

Soon enough, the day was over and not much else had happened. Mollie had unpacked all the boxes in the kitchen and the living room; she'd put the Steeles' things away in places that seemed right to her—she'd learned from the best, after all, her mother being the true expert on household organization—and there wasn't anything else for her to do short of going upstairs and getting into their personal stuff, which she was not inclined to do just then. She did look in on Sarah, stood at the door and peered at her, but she was sleeping, a vague shape in the bed, with Plato curled up beside her. Mollie tried banging around a bit, hoping Sarah might wake up and thank her and pay her and invite her to stay for dinner. She'd have been happy to cook for them. She could picture them all sitting together there at the table, just like old times. But Sarah didn't wake up, and then Mollie figured that in her delicate condition she needed her rest and probably wouldn't have any appetite anyway. Better for everybody to take it easy, hold back, and play it slow, one day at a time.

So she made her way back up to the house on the

hill by herself, and she was still thinking that maybe it was going to all be okay.

Even as exhausted as she was, Mollie didn't sleep much that night. She tossed and turned in her little attic room, caught someplace in the shadows between waking and dreaming, picturing what it must have been like for the Molenes to suddenly not be themselves anymore.

First of all, just after it happened, when they left the Grotto, they would have had no idea where they lived. Deek and Emily didn't even know the Steeles; they'd only just met them for the first time that day, and now they *were* the Steeles. That had to be a shock. Deek would have had to look in his wallet for identification; he'd have had to look at his own driver's license, probably happy to notice that now he didn't even need his glasses to read the small print. But of course, the license wasn't going to tell him anything because John and Sarah had just moved to Brevity and so the address on it would have been in someplace else altogether. Deek was also likely to have noticed that John had been born in the late 1960's, and it would have been another shock for him to realize that he himself was in his fifties then, his own life already more than halfway gone. He would look up to see his wife walking off, steady on her feet now, hips swaying in a way that they hadn't swayed in years, heading purposefully for the pay phone on the corner, where she would call information and use her young voice to flirt with the operator, cajoling him into giving her the correct address for the Steeles.

Let's say that in the meantime Deek sees that some guys are playing a game of basketball in the lot across the street, and he jaywalks over to lean against the low brick wall and watch. The game is fierce; the players tumble back and forth over the court, knocking into each other, sweating, grunting, calling out. Deek takes off his jacket. He unknots his tie, rolls up his sleeves. Flexes his hands. Vaults the wall and joins in the game, and now he's running, bumping into other players, stealing the ball, dribbling, faking, shooting, lost for a while in the ease and energy of his young body and what must be the pure pleasure of simply being himself. He hears a voice calling his name, and he looks up to see Sarah Steele, haloed by the lamplight. He turns away from the game and walks back into the shadows toward her. He is sweating, winded, but alive!

"I have the address," Sarah says. "We live up on Bridge Street."

He puts his arm around her, and they begin to

walk. It's late by this time, and the evening movies are just letting out. The rain has stopped, and in this college town, there are young people everywhere, walking and talking, laughing, standing in groups, sitting at outdoor tables, drinking cappuccino, eating ice cream. In their new bodies, Deek and Emily move unnoticed among the others. They look pretty much like everybody else.

"We did it, Em," Deek says.

"I know."

"We're not going to die."

She stops and looks at him. "Not yet."

"Isn't it marvelous?" he exclaims. "Just look at all the life here. The streets are teeming with it. Even the sky, swarming with stars, all burning furiously, flaming, full of fire. That's me, Em. I'm like that, too. Still burning. Still clinging to my own small flame."

She reaches for him; he draws her up and holds her close. They stand together as one unit, stationary in a river of people, buffeted by the surging crowd.

And then when they find the Steeles' house, he uses the keys he's found in his pocket to open the front door. He steps back while Emily goes in before him. She stops and turns, gives him a look of worried expectation. What now? Slowly, he approaches her. Tenderly, he touches her. Gently, he brings her close.

All his love for her is welling up inside him. And hers for him in her. They have all the time in the world to learn each other all over again. They kiss, and they know: this is right. Deek and Emily, here they are, and they belong together still.

He pulls away and looks into her eyes, then takes her hand and turns, and she follows him through the house, up the stairs to bed.

While outside the window, a siren wails, and the flashing red light washes the walls as the ambulance speeds past, on its way up the hill to the Molenes'.

Slowly, sexily, a young woman named Sarah Steele is slipping out of her dress.

While an old lady known as Emily Molene struggles with an EMT who wants her to calm down.

A man named John unbuttons his shirt, takes it off, unbuckles his belt, steps out of his pants.

While the unmoving and unconscious body of Deek Molene is transferred from a gurney to a bed.

John and Sarah move toward each other. Their bodies are healthy, their flesh is strong and young and beautiful, and they are flushed with desire.

Emily feels the sting of a needle, and then everything goes black.

Sarah falls into John's arms; he rolls her down onto her back; he opens her up; she takes him in.

The respirator whooshes air into Deek's lungs; a heart monitor keeps time. Emily sleeps, drugged and mercifully unaware.

And Mollie, she's on her cot in the attic; it's a couple of days later, and she's dreaming this up, imagining her way into it, and that's when it hits her. That's when she realizes what all of this really means: that Deek and Emily, the real Deek and Emily, the ones who have turned into John and Sarah Steele, they just want her to go away and leave them alone. To them now, she's not an angel anymore; she's an inconvenience. They can pretend that she is nobody. They can pretend that she is nothing. They can make believe they never knew her, or loved her, or needed her. To them now, she might just as well have never been at all.

That was the lowest point for Mollie. Never before in her whole life had she felt so all alone.

The next morning, Mollie was waiting in the shadows of the Molenes' front porch when Sarah Steele came by on her daily run. How Emily must have loved that! So steady on her feet, and no more aches and pains. Mollie's intention was to ambush her, but Sarah had brought Plato along on a leash, and when he saw Mollie, he started barking at her like she was a stranger or something and he was protecting his mistress, which was completely unnecessary.

To her credit, Sarah did stop and apologize about the dog, who must have come back to the house sometime the night before, but when Mollie started to explain that she knew what had happened, Sarah got this worried look on her face, which made Mollie want to explain more about how it was cool with her, she was happy for her, for them, but she was also hoping that they still had some room left in their lives for her? She must have come off pretty desperate, but Sarah kept acting like she didn't know what Mollie was talking about, and so she kept on trying to explain, finally just coming out with it that she knew she was pregnant and everything and that she completely understood how important that was to her, but what she was doing was really wrong if you stopped to think about it, taking somebody else's whole life and turning it into your own.

By this time, Sarah was starting to back away. She said she had to go, that it was nice talking to her, but she had to go, and then she flashed her smile and turned and went back to her running, and Mollie didn't think she had any choice but to go after her, so maybe it looked like she was chasing her or something, and then Sarah stopped again and told her to please, leave her alone or she would have to call the police.

Mollie was not used to running like that. She was sweaty and out of breath, and so maybe it was hard for Sarah to understand what she was trying to tell her because she stopped her cold. Put up a hand and snapped Mollie's name, loudly and with force, the way her mother used to do when she wanted her to shut up for a minute and pay attention.

Then, she started telling Mollie about what she'd been hearing about her. That she had a reputation. That people were saying she was troubled. That it was obvious she needed help and maybe she should go to Student Health and talk to someone there. Somebody who was trained to handle situations like this.

And Mollie started to argue back that she didn't think there was anybody on the planet who'd been trained to handle anything like this, but then Plato was barking at her again, and Sarah turned and was once more running away, dragging him along with her, and then they had rounded the corner and were gone.

Mollie realized then that her last hope was to try to talk some sense into Deek since he'd always been the more rational one of the two anyway. She found him in John's office—in John's body—and Mouse's Ex was there with him, sitting on the edge of his desk, swinging her leg, batting her eyes, asking him about the open mike reading that night and what did he think she should bring to read, or should she read at all? Mollie stood in the doorway for a second until he looked up at her with John's green eyes and ironic smirk, but his performance was perfect, it was right on the money; he looked straight through her, like she wasn't even there, or like he'd never seen her before in his life, and even the Ex noticed because she turned to see what he was looking at, even as she kept on talking, and then he went back to listening to her and she turned back to face him and Mollie understood that she might have been nobody for all that he seemed to care.

So that was it then. They had their youth back. They had each other. Mollie was nothing to them anymore.

But that was so ungrateful, wasn't it? It was so unfair. Mom says, "Life isn't fair, Mollie." Dad says, "Get used to it." This was Emily and Deek's new beginning. It was their fresh start, their own kind of a commencement into a second chance at life. With no place in it for anybody else.

We could say that that's when Mollie stopped feeling sorry for herself. We could say that that's when she started to get mad.

The only thing that Mollie could think to do then was to go back to the hospital. She wanted to see Emily and Deek for herself, if only to make sure that she was right. She took out her nose ring, and she removed the ear studs. She gelled her crazy hair down flat, and she put on her best white uniform, and then she climbed the hill and pushed in through the front door. She just walked right past the front desk, past the waiting room, past the old Coot at Information, straight down the hall and around the corner to the elevators that would take her up to Intensive Care on the fourth floor. No more Little Miss Scaredy-cat, no more weepy granddaughter, no more helpless little girl. Mollie fell into her role of nurse and acted like it was no big deal, like this was just something she did every day, like she actually knew her way around, like she really did belong there. She even smiled and nodded and said hello to some of the people that she passed—an orderly pushing an empty gurney, another nurse like herself, even an old guy in blue scrubs who looked like he might have been a surgeon—as if she knew them and they were supposed to know her in return. And sure enough, they acted like they did. That's the way to get things done, Postscript always said. Just pretend you know what you're doing, and everybody is going to assume that you really do, even if you don't have a clue. Most people are lazy that way, he said. They're the ones who see a long line and get right in it, even when they aren't sure what it's for. They just take it for granted that everybody else knows something they don't know, and they don't want to be caught with their pants off and their ignorance showing. Postscript wasn't even thirteen years old yet when Mollie first got to know him back in Nowhere—he was still just a kid and too young to already have become so philosophical about things. But his father and stepmother's mistreatment of him had turned that boy into a cynic and a blanket even wetter than Mollie's own dad, and that was maybe the worst consequence of the hole left inside him from the innocence he had lost to them.

It's not hard to find the I.C.U. because there are signs all over the place announcing its location and warning everybody who doesn't belong there to "Keep Out!" "Authorized Personnel Only!" "No Visitors!"

Mollie blows right past those, though, and finds a place to stand beside Deek's bed, and once she's in position she knows she's not going to have much time before somebody comes along and catches her there and starts asking questions that she has no idea how to answer, so she leans in close to his face, or at least as close as she can get anyway, what with all the wires and tubes and pumps that he's hooked up to. She's expecting him to smell bad, but he doesn't. She's thinking there's going to be an odor of decay about him, the way her grandfather's feet always smelled like old pot roast when he took off his shoes, but there is nothing like that here, only the eye-stinging stink of rubbing alcohol in a cold void of over-oxygenated air.

She says his name. "John?" And waits for a reaction, but there's nothing. She tries again. "John Steele?" She's thinking that all she needs is a signal of some kind. Just one little indication to show her that he really is in there somewhere, and then she'll know for sure that she's doing the right thing. The pump whooshes and the heart monitor beeps, but there's nothing else, and in its stillness Deek's body looks like it's already dead.

She closes her eyes and thinks, hard, tries to read his mind, tries to call out to him. Tries to contact him, trying so hard it feels like her head might be about to explode, steam coming out of her ears, like a cartoon, her face flushed with the effort of it. She's doing all that she can do, copying her Aunt Lucy, but her mind is racing, jumping all over the place, she can't hold it, can't focus. And then she remembers. She's not supposed to be reading his thoughts, finding John Steele in there somewhere; she's supposed to be sending hers. This is much simpler. She sits down. Relaxes. Looks at him, calmly. The sounds of the pumps and the machines, whirring and burping and sighing and beeping—she uses it as a sort of music that she can play to, a sort of one-man band to send out a message to him. She stares at him, hard, and begs him, if you are John Steele, all you have to do is tell me. Just say so. Give me a sign. Wiggle a finger. Blink an eye. Do something. She watches carefully. Tell me, she thinks. Just tell me.

Nothing. His breathing. The pump. His eyes aren't even moving. He's not dreaming. He's gone.

Or so she thinks. Until the machine starts to beep wildly, for no good reason at all. Mollie jumps to her feet, leans over him, "John!" but is brushed aside by the nurse who has rushed in. Several hospital workers swarm the door, coming to his aid. Mollie is ushered out, and she stands in the hallway while they work on him.

Here come the tears again. Mollie slaps them away. She has to be strong about this because if she does what she knows she's going to have to do, her old friend Deek Molene is going to have to die. But if she doesn't, if she lets him stay, if she leaves it alone and forgets about it, then John Steele is going to be the one who dies instead, and won't that be partly her fault? For allowing it to happen? For not stopping it when she had the chance? Could she live with herself for the long rest of her own whole life knowing that she's the kind of person who could just turn and walk away from a thing like this as if it didn't have anything at all to do with her?

Here's a fact: everybody back home in Nowhere knew what those people who called themselves his parents were doing to Postscript, and not one person lifted a finger to try and stop them, not one person said, "Hey, wait a minute, this isn't right." Not the neighbors, not the teachers, not the cops... nobody. Not even Mollie herself. So nobody should have been a bit surprised by it later when they brought him back again and he finally did what he did, when Postscript did just exactly what he had to do to get out.

http://www.badideas.com/mwvbmb.html
How to Build a Microwave Bomb
by Terminator

IMPORTANT NOTICE TO ALL CONCERNED: Certain text files and messages contained on this website deal with activities and devices which would be in violation of various Federal, State, and local laws if actually carried out or constructed. The webmasters of this site do not advocate the breaking of any law. Our text files and message bases are for informational purposes only. We recommend that you contact your local law enforcement officials before undertaking any project based upon any information obtained from this or any other web site. We do not guarantee that any of the information contained on this system is correct, workable, or factual. We are not responsible for, nor do we assume any liability for, damages resulting from the use of any information on this site.

So you're bored and you want to make a simple but effective bomb without messing with liquids or powder stuff? This one doesn't take a rocket scientist to create. Actually, my eight-year-old brother can do this.

MATERIALS:

Microwave. A used one is best unless you want to mess up your mom's brand new one! You can find them at tag sales for about ten dollars, and as long as it works, you are fine.

Duct tape. Get this at any store.

Spray cans. About three of these, depending on

how big the microwave is. You might be able to fit more.

(Optional) Batteries. Size D, as many as you want.

PROCEDURE:

You need to plug the microwave into an electrical outlet. (Tip: NOT AT YOUR HOME!! Unless that's what you're planning to blow up, which is sick.) I recommend getting a very damn long cable extension and plugging it into your electrical outlet.

Place the microwave where you want the explosion to take place.

Next, take the spray cans and shove them into the microwave. Make sure the door is shut tight.

Now, get the duct tape and wrap it tightly around the whole thing. (Tip: Avoid covering the buttons on the microwave, as you will need to punch in some numbers later on.)

After you're done wrapping the whole thing with duct tape, punch in the highest temperature on the microwave and get your ass out of there because:

KA-FUCKING-BOOM!!!

[This will make a pretty damn big explosion, but

if that still doesn't make you happy, you can add the size "D" batteries to make it blow up with a much greater force.]

P.S. I am not responsible for your stupid ass actions, so don't blame Terminator for any of these acts you carry on.

(Of course, Postscript thought this guy Terminator was speaking directly to him.)

We sincerely hope that now maybe people are going to be able to understand that Mollie didn't really have any choice anymore, knowing what she knew, and seeing what she'd seen—that it was up to her to fix this situation, to make it right again. Nobody else was going to do it. You could say she was desperate, but that's not exactly true. Because desperation makes you think of somebody who's at the end of their rope, somebody who is crazy, somebody who will do anything, and Mollie wasn't crazy then, any more than she is crazy now. She wasn't even hectic; she was very, very calm. For the first time in a while, she felt like she was finally in control. Of herself anyway. Because she knew exactly what she had to do.

And so, still in her uniform, she left the hospital

and rode the bus out to the Wal-Mart to get the things she'd need. The Ping-Pong balls, the duct tape, three boxes of strike-anywhere matches, six bright bottles of nail polish, two jars of Pyrodex, and the Bic. There was no reason to buy sandpaper; she wouldn't be throwing her bombs to make them go off. And after she'd messed her hair back up and put the rings and studs in where they belonged, then she started to feel like she was finally getting back to being something like her old self again.

She found the display of Sarah's Heart Strings greeting cards in the party section with the gift wrap and ribbons and balloons. She just stood there for a while, reading them, every one, letting them tug away at her. Sentimental old sap, she fell apart, right there in the store, slobbering all over herself and getting a look from a pig-nosed sales clerk, who had been hovering nearby, fiddling with a display of plastic photo cubes. Mollie glared back at her and sniffed and snapped "What?" loudly enough to embarrass both of them and make the other turn away. When the clerk returned to offer Mollie a Kleenex a moment later, as well as a box of Band-Aids for the scratches on her arms, the kindness of the gesture just about killed her, but she managed to say thank you and pull herself back together, pay for her stuff and get on the bus again, heading back to the Molenes' house one last time to change her clothes, put together her necklace, get the magic goblets, and head down to Stanley Hall.

CHAPTER EIGHT

Now we've come to the part of the story that everybody probably already knows, the part that (thanks to Doyle Hirleman and his video camera) was played over and over again on the news: i.e., what happened at the Open Mike reading that night. They held the event in the now-famous room that was known as "the little aud," on the third floor of Stanley Hall. It was really nothing more than a classroom with a curtained wall at one end, behind a low platform stage that was highlighted by a bank of lights hanging from a scaffold overhead. A miked lectern and a tall stool had been set up for the readers along with a small table equipped with a water pitcher and some paper cups. Several rows of folding metal chairs were arranged in haphazard rows, but they were mostly empty. There wasn't much of an audience that night, just the faculty, who were required to be there—they must have been, why else would they have come?—a few readers, and some of their friends. The whole thing was supposed to start at 7:30, but Mollie got there a few minutes late, so she was able to slip in the door and find a place to stand at the back without calling too much attention to herself before the overhead lights went out. She'd put Deek's long raincoat on over her dress anyway, and her sneakers on her feet in case she had to do any running, so with the coat closed, she looked pretty normal, she thought. She'd put her gear into a backpack, and that she was carrying that looked normal, too.

First, Dr. Phillips got up to speak, and he was in full performance mode, squinting past the lights at the audience, tapping the mike, taking a sip of water, pulling at his goatee. He started out by welcoming everybody, and then, he explained the rules. Readings were to be five minutes long, tops. The Fabricunt had a timer and a bell that she was supposed to start ringing if anybody went over the limit. She raised these items to show the crowd and then shook her shoulders, shivering all over with the thrill of having been chosen to assist Dr. Phillips along with the delicious power of the job that he'd asked her to do. It was right up her alley, shutting people up. Each reader was supposed to introduce the next one, reading from the signup list that had been taped to the top of the lectern—name and title and genre—and then, Dr. Phillips went on, "If there's time and anybody else wants to read after the list has been exhausted, just raise your hand, and you are welcome to come up here and let us hear what you have to say." Big goat smile, smattering of applause while he cleared his throat, leaned closer to the mike, and got serious.

A moment of silence, and then, he was talking about the Molenes, explaining about their collapse before going on to describe how Deek had first founded this department back in 1955. He was asking that everyone keep the old folks in their prayers, or if that wasn't appropriate, at least in their thoughts. The Widow was sitting in the front row, a jangling black shape, and there in the second row, on the far left, sat John and Sarah Steele. Mollie pushed away from the back wall and crept up closer to take a seat in an empty chair behind them. The Steeles were leaning forward, listening intently to this tribute to the Molenes. Paying full attention. Eyes and ears peeled. John had hold of Sarah's hand, and he was squeezing it while she took a deep breath and sighed. Mollie counted this as further evidence that she was right.

Doyle had set up his camera to the right of the stage, and Mouse was nearby, apparently keeping an eye on the sound levels. Neither of them noticed Mollie, and she was grateful for that.

First on stage was a guy with a scraggly beard reciting a poem about climbing a tree to watch his mom's best friend swimming naked in her backyard pool. Then, an overweight girl in a T-shirt and miniskirt and shit-kicker boots read an essay about stealing money from her brother to buy pot from her dad. This one seemed too long, and the audience was stirring when finally Fabricunt jumped up and rang her bell, and the Shitkicker, furious at having been interrupted, stomped off the stage. On and on it went—a novel excerpt about drag queens drag racing, a story where a kid is telling his teacher about a dead calf he found out in a field, another one that's narrated by a dog, a poem about a woman arranging flowers and thinking about blowing the bagboy at the grocery store. On and on and on, and Mollie was getting sleepy, and sweating in her clothes and the coat, she started to nod off when Fabricunt began ringing that bell again, and everyone was applauding, and Dr. Phillips was back up there at the mike, hand shading his eyes as he peered past the lights at the audience and asked: "Who wants to be next?"

She was on her feet and out of her chair and on the stage before anybody else had a chance to respond.

The room went quiet. She leaned toward the mike and said, too loudly, "My name is Mollie Mifflin." Smatter of polite applause, and Dr. Phillips sat back down.

First, she digs into the backpack, pulls out the goblets, sets them on the table next to the paper cups. They look exquisite under the lights, and a murmur of wonder can be heard, moving through the audience. Next, she brings out the book and opens it to the place that she's marked. Into the mike again, she says: "I'm going to be reading a short passage from the greatest novel ever written." Another murmur from the audience, but Mollie only smiles. Finally, she shrugs off the coat. And when they see what she's wearing, there is a gasp…

This is how it looks in Doyle's film: there's this girl on a lit stage, and she's wearing a wedding dress and high top black sneakers. She's crazy-looking, with her hair sticking out all over her head and a string of about fifty painted Ping-Pong balls—Brandy Alexander, Cranberry Red, Aruba Blue, California Coral, Eighteen Carrot, Key Lime Crush, Plumberry, and Pink Lemonade—wrapped in several layers around her neck. The dress is vintage 1940's: a ball gown with a full net skirt spun from silver thread and an iridescent bodice shimmering in sequins.

This girl, she really is an angel. And this Angel, she begins to read from *Forevermore*, the part where Frances tells her daughter that she will do anything for her, the part where she explains about loyalty and sacrifice and the total selflessness of unconditional love.

"Remember that?" the Angel asks.

She is looking past the lights now, at someone in the crowd. She steps off the stage, reaches into the darkness, and pulls Sarah Steele to her feet and up into the spotlight with her. "Emily," she says. She does a little turn, fingertips flaring the netting of her skirt. "Do you recognize the dress?"

Sarah seems baffled. "I don't..."

The Angel pushes the Ping-Pong balls aside—they clatter against each other dangerously—and she fishes around in the bosom of her bodice, pulls out a card, and hands it to Sarah, who looks at it as if she's never seen anything like it before. On the front: A heart, fat and swollen, full to bursting, pulsing with smears of deep red and dark purple, afloat on a seething sea of yellow flames.

The Angel nods, encouragingly. "Read it," she whispers.

Sarah clears her throat. She turns to the crowd and reads: "If I know what love is, it is because of you." She looks up. "Herman Hesse."

The Angel is smiling; she is as patient and kindly as Glinda. "You have to go back now, Emily," she says. Tears sparkle in her eyes. "You know that, don't you?"

Sarah frowns. Shakes her head.

The Angel says, "It's over now," then reaches for her, puts her arms around her, pulls her close, breathes in the sweet, familiar fragrance of rosewater and whispers, "I love you, Emily. I'll never forget you. You changed my life. And I promise, I will always be your own good girl. Forevermore."

By this time, John has leaped to his feet, and the Fabricunt is frantically ringing her bell while Dr. Phillips has stepped forward and seems about to interfere, but the Angel has her lighter in her hand, and she flicks it. It flames. She holds it forth, and they all stop.

"In case you're wondering about my necklace," the Angel says, "it's a bomb." And then she explains about how each Ping-Pong ball is packed with match heads and Pyrodex, strung together into a chain of cherry bombs, and all she has to do is light one and they'll all go off one by one—if not killing her, then at least making a big terrible mess. "We don't want that to happen," she says. "Do we?"

Sarah asks, "What do you want?"

It's so simple. "I want you to wish yourselves back."

She picks up the goblets and hands the woman one to Sarah. She beckons to John. She waves the lighter at Dr. Phillips, who is trying to move closer, and shouts, "Stay the fuck back! I mean it, get back!"

Then sweetly, to John. "Please."

Mollie is holding the goblet out for him to take. He steps onto the stage and stands beside his wife. They exchange a nervous glance. Fabricunt gapes at them, her mouth hanging open, speechless for once. Mouse, standing to the side, seems to be thinking that this is all just some kind of crazy stunt, and she likes it. Her arms are folded over her chest, and she doesn't look afraid, she looks amused. Doyle's movie camera churns.

Now, the Angel pours water from the pitcher into each of the goblets.

She nods to Sarah and John. "You know what to do," she says.

They hesitate, look at each other, then at the goblets.

The Angel commands: "Drink!"

Sarah lifts hers, takes a sip. John does the same.

Silence.

The Widow can be heard asking, "What's happening?"

The Angel looks mystified. "Hold on a second..."

A moment of hesitation, a whisper of self-doubt, and that's all it takes for Dr. Phillips to decide he wants to be a hero. He rushes forward to tackle Mollie and knock the lighter out of her hand. There's a scuffle as some of the others in the audience jump to their feet and surge forward, too. Chairs clatter to the floor behind them.

But the Angel is prepared. The Angel is fast. She's quick and lithe, and before anyone can stop her, she is standing on the tall stool, holding her lighter aloft.

Dr. Phillips hesitates. He steps back and knocks against John, who jostles Sarah, who releases the goblet in her hand. It somersaults slowly away from her, seems to hang for a moment in the air where it dazzles in the light, before it falls, tumbling, cracks against the edge of the platform, and shatters on the floor.

What happened next was Mollie ordered everybody out, she told them all to leave, including Doyle and his camera, and Dr. Phillips and Mouse and Fabricunt and the Widow. The Shitkicker, the Treeclimber, the Calfboy, the Dragqueen, the Flowergirl and the Talking Dog. Everybody! Out! Now!

At first, she thought that maybe she was wrong,

maybe she'd made mistake. Maybe John and Sarah Steele really were only that, John and Sarah Steele. Maybe the goblets didn't grant wishes. Maybe Deek and Emily were simply old and dying, as they should, as they must. At first, she felt so stupid. This whole bomb thing—it was just a way to get their attention, that's all. To get them to listen. To get them to do what needed to be done. How else was somebody like Mollie Mifflin supposed to take charge of a situation that was already so far out of control?

The room was empty; she was alone. The female goblet was on the floor, her bowl shattered, her body in shards. Mollie bent and picked up one piece, tried to fit it to another, but it was impossible. She sat down and cradled the bits and pieces in the shimmery silver netting of her skirt in her lap.

The Principle of Parsimony. This was something else that Mr. Whitley had explained, what now seemed like a lifetime ago. Occam's Razor, he called it. Which says: always choose the simplest explanation of a phenomenon in order to find the solution that requires the fewest leaps of logic. She was thinking: but what if that was wrong? For example, the simplest solution to the problem of her mother's life had been for her to get rid of everybody in it. The simplest solution to the problem of Postscript's treatment by his family was to ignore it. The simplest solution to the problem of getting old is to stop aging and die.

All right then, she thought, just because the goblets didn't come to life when John and Sarah drank from them, that didn't necessarily mean that they weren't magic. In fact, if you looked at it that way, it actually proved that they were. Because the goblets only grant one wish. And John and Sarah Steele were not really John and Sarah Steele; they were Deek and Emily Molene. And Deek and Emily Molene had already made their wish—to be young again—so they couldn't have another one. The only people who could make that wish together were John and Sarah Steele, who had become Deek and Emily Molene, who had not yet made a wish of their own.

But Deek and Emily Molene, who were really John and Sarah Steele, couldn't make a wish either because they were in the hospital, and he was unconscious and Mollie didn't even know where she was or whether she could find her, which she didn't think she could because that would have meant she'd have to somehow get out of Stanley Hall and go to the hospital and get to Emily's room, and now there were cops all over the place outside, and there was no way that they were going to let Mollie go anywhere, not with a bomb around her neck. Not after what she'd done.

And besides, one of the goblets was broken.

Campus police were called first, but it didn't take them long to realize that the situation was out of their league, and so they were soon joined by city cops, who evacuated the rest of the building and blocked the streets and cordoned off the area all around it. Mollie had had some contact with them right from the start by way of the telephone there in the department office, and the kindly-seeming detective with the deep voice was trying to be patient with her, but he had a job to do and he wanted her to make no mistake—he was not amused.

By then, she had moved out of Old Aud and into Dr. Phillips's private office in the corner of the building because that had good clear view of the parking lot below so she could keep an eye on what was going on out there. The cops could see her standing in the window, too, and so right away they were calling her. Postscript would have advised her not to answer, but she couldn't resist. How difficult it is for a girl to turn away from a man who wants to talk to her. Vanity, again.

They tried to tell her that her mother was on the line, but Mollie didn't believe that for a second because how did they get Mrs. Mifflin's phone number? Mollie wouldn't have talked to her mother anyway, even if she was on the line, even if she was begging her daughter to turn herself in, even if it sounded like she cared, promising to get her help, a doctor or a lawyer or whatever, no matter how much it cost, even if she told her she was going to do all she could to get her out of this mess she was in.

They must have thought she was stupid.

The nice man with the deep voice asks her, "Don't you even want to talk to your mother, Mollie?"

Mollie replies, "No, sir, I don't."

She went on to tell him, in no uncertain terms, that if the cops made one false move, if they tried anything funny, she would not hesitate to do what she had to do and blow those balls to smithereens. Make a name for herself that way, not to mention an unpleasant mess that somebody else was going to have to come in and clean up. And also not to mention giving Doyle Hirleman a brilliant ending for his film. Mollie was just hoping, for everybody's sake, that they were taking her seriously.

She was finding Dr. Phillips's office to be a suitably comfortable place for holing up and hiding out. Plush sofa, solid desk, nice brass lamp, and expensive-looking Persian rug. The chair was real leather, and in the closet, there was a sort of mini-bar with chips and nuts and whiskey and a pint-sized refrigerator stocked with an opened bottle of white wine, some cans of beer, a Coke, and a couple of packages of cheese. She figured she could make herself at home there for a while, if she had to.

Dr. Phillips also had created a sort of a shrine in his office, to himself and to his work. It was there to impress his students, especially the new ones, this display of his own first editions, translations, awards, photographs, and autographs, the works. Plus, he had gathered there what he claimed to be a priceless collection of rare books and manuscripts by other authors, all of them many times more famous than he was ever likely to be, and most of them already dead. For example, he had a bound folio edition of Geoffrey Chaucer's *Works* and a 1952 first edition of *East of Eden* by John Steinbeck, plus first editions of the four novels of Lawrence Durrell's *The Alexandria Quartet*. There was also an inscribed 1934 first edition presentation copy of *Goodbye, Mr. Chips* by James Hilton and a 1903 first edition of Jack London's *The Call of the Wild.* Together these books formed an impressive part of the "phallocentric Western canon"—according to Mouse Wendler, which made Doyle Hirleman smile and roll his baby-blues at her when she said it. Phillips kept them in a glass case with a lock on it—

one that turned out to be pretty flimsy, but this was Iowa, so maybe he hadn't been expecting anything but good clean honest milk-fed admiration, not larceny or extortion or any other forms of criminal intent.

Mollie isn't half the lock-picker that Postscript is, but it only took her about two minutes to break into the case and get her hands on the goods, and then she propped them up on the windowsill for everybody to see, in case the authorities had any doubts about the seriousness of her intentions. She wanted to put them on alert that she was holding those works hostage. She was banking on her belief that Dr. Phillips was not going to let anybody blow bullet holes in the covers, risk shredding the paper with pieces of plastic shrapnel from a bomb, or blot the precious words and pictures with messy bits of a girl's own gynocentric flesh and blood.

Almost immediately, the campus and Brevity cops tried to close off the Springer campus to keep onlookers away, but because of the open layout of the buildings, as well as the limited resources of the police, this turned out to be next to impossible.

As news of Mollie's siege spread—fed as it was by the live television coverage and the deliberately concocted rumors of some assorted political interests—

more and more people, from the town of Brevity as well as outlying communities as far away as Des Moines to the north and Linwood to the west—began to pour into the area. Soon the crowd numbered in the thousands, and the scene became festive as vendors set up food stalls and opportunistic demonstrators held up banners, chanted slogans, waved signs. Among the groups participating in the flash-mob that had spontaneously generated itself, like frogs in a mud puddle, were The Center for the Advancement of Non-Violence, Students for Violent Non-Action, PETA, NARAL, The Ruckus Society, MADD, The Anti-Fluoride Coalition, Food First, Just Act, and The Rainforest Action Network, among many others.

Mollie stood at the window, raised her fist, and the crowd went wild. Soon, she thought, there would be T-shirts and baseball caps and coffee mugs with her face on the front. Nobody is Somebody now.

The situation developed into a full-out stand-off when several people, supporting Mollie, managed to break through the police barriers and plant themselves just outside the building's outer doors, proclaiming themselves to be human shields, protecting her from what they feared would be an armed assault that could only end badly for everyone. She continued to talk to the kind man with the deep voice—and hopes were high that the situation could be nonviolently resolved. Meanwhile, a local band had set up its equipment in the parking lot, and the whole thing was turning into a party out there. Whenever Mollie showed herself at the window, the crowd went wild. They could see that she was still wearing the Ping-Pong balls. After a while, she turned off the lights and left them to imagine what might be about to happen next.

The mob began to dwindle then, as people settled down for the night or simply drifted away. Some were in it for the long run, though, and they rolled out sleeping bags and set up tents. The human shields remained in place outside the building's doors. The police seemed to be regrouping. A fire truck was parked in the middle of the street, forcing traffic to find another route through to the other side of town. There was a feeling of expectation in the air but also a sense of seriousness, sobriety, patience, even a sort of preternatural calm. Nobody wanted Mollie to be hurt. Nobody wanted the scene to get ugly. Nobody wanted the police to decide to use force to get her to do what they wanted her to do—give up, come out, turn herself in. Some people sang peace songs. Others knelt together and prayed.

As for Mollie, she knew what she had to do. Occam's Razor this time, straight to the point. One person. One goblet. One wish.

Here's a happy ending for you:

Deek and Emily, they had a good life together, but it was time for them to go. John and Sarah Steele, their story had only just begun.

And Mollie? There she went...

Happily ever after...

The end.

Kaboom.

She takes off the collar and puts all the books back where they belong. She pours some wine into the one remaining goblet, and she sips. Swallows. Sips again, just in case. She closes her eyes and waits. She is so tired, and at the same time hyped up, her ears are ringing.

"Someone has said your name," her mother used to tell her when this happened, and for a long time now that someone has been Horace. "Mollie?" She opens her eyes and sees that the goblet has begun to glow. The ringing has become a sort of buzzing, and the buzzing is getting louder. The goblet is moving now, too; it's softening, like wax.

And then, just like that, the little man is alive. Not glass anymore. Flesh and blood. But small.

Ha! Just like in the book, Mollie thinks. Ha! Now, she is seeing it for herself.

He puts down his fluted bowl, rubs his hands together, and looks around. Then, he stops, and with his fists on his hips, he is peering up at her. "Where is she?" he asks.

Mollie winces at that. Guilty.

She starts apologizing. "Oh God, I'm sorry," she tells him. "I'm really sorry. But it wasn't my fault." She starts to explain. "See, Dr. Phillips——"

But he cuts her off. Waves his hands around. Wants to know, more forcefully: "Where is she?"

So she tells him the truth. Takes responsibility. Comes clean. "She broke."

Not what he wants to hear. "What do you mean she broke?"

She goes, "I mean someone dropped her. I mean she fell. Shattered."

"Shattered?"

"A million pieces," she tells him. "Smithereens."

The little guy shakes his head. "Oh, man..."

She asks him, "Can't you give me a wish without her?"

He looks at her like she's the village idiot. He asks her again. "Where is she?"

She picks up the sheet of paper where she's put the pieces of the broken goblet and sets it down near him on the desk. He walks around it, nudging a hand and then a leg with his bare foot.

"Hey," she warns him. "Be careful." She doesn't want him to cut himself.

But he doesn't even look at her. He just shakes his head. Says, "Ugh, what a mess."

He goes to work, picking up the pieces, hauling them here and there until they are an approximate assemblage of his mate. He stands back then and surveys his work. And sure enough, the pieces start to glow just as he did, and they soften too, and then just like that, there she is. They've melded together to form the little woman, and she is wholly herself again, only the smallest nicks of nothingness on her body here and there.

She stands up, stretching, feeling stiff it seems.

She asks, "What happened?"

The small man tips his chin to Mollie. "Clumsy girl," he says.

She starts to explain again that it wasn't her fault, but he waves her away. And so she tells them, "I need my wish now."

The man raises his hand, shakes two fingers at her. "Two people. You know the rules."

Mollie argues. "I have a brother."

"So what?"

"His name is Horace."

The man is shaking his head.

"He's here. In me."

He thinks about this.

"Plus, there's only one goblet now. You have to do it for one."

He looks at the small woman. "You up to it?" he asks. She shrugs. "I guess."

And so that's how they did it. Mollie and Horace fixed it. She closed her eyes and crossed her fingers, and together they made the wish and put everybody back where they belonged.

The rest of the story you may already know. It's a part of the public record; it was on the local news and in the local papers, and it has become legend on the Springer College campus, too. But in case you missed it, and to bring some closure to the chain of events as we've described them here, this is what happens next:

The authorities outside have already moved in to arrest the handful of human shields outside the doors of the building. They use a megaphone to tell Mollie that unless she surrenders herself to them immediately, they're going to have to come in and forcibly remove her from the premises. When there's no response to this, the cops regroup and begin to move forward. A woman's voice is heard to shriek: "Waco!" And this is echoed by someone else: "Waco!" And from that the chant is taken up by the rest of the mob: "Waco! Waco!"

Undeterred, the police continue their advance on the building, but before they're able to make entry into it, a series of several loud explosions shook the air, and puffs of smoke can be seen emanating from the open window of Dr. Phillips' corner office. The chanting stops, the police draw back their forces, and everybody waits. A murmur begins to move through the crowd; then, it deepens into a kind of collective moan.

There follows another loud crackle of multiple explosions, and the woman who shrieked before is wailing now. Almost immediately her cry is first joined and then overwhelmed by the rising howl of the building's fire alarm. Several people will be heard to say later that the sound of this was so unexpected and so deafening it felt like the end of the world.

The news footage shows some movement at the entrance to the building, and after a long moment, a figure emerges from the darkened doorway. She staggers out into the daylight. She has what's left of the bomb collar in one hand, and she is still got up in the old wedding dress, but now her bright hair is dark and wet and plastered to her head. Her black high tops squelch as she takes a couple of steps forward, then stops. She tosses the collar onto the grass, where it lies coiled like a ruined snake.

She raises both arms high over her head, in a clear gesture of surrender, and wiggles her hips. The silvery netting of the dress's skirt sends off a spray of shimmery sparks.

Water. She is soaking wet, because the sprinkler system went off and doused the fire, doused the books, doused her.

She is holding something in her hand.

The police draw their guns and aim them at her.

The megaphone blares, a man's deep voice: "Freeze!" and she does.

"Drop your weapon!"

She blinks and frowns and shakes her head and says something, but it's impossible to hear her over the sound of the fire alarm, which is still wailing.

"Mollie Mifflin!" the megaphone blares again. "Drop your weapon! Do it now!"

She shakes her head again, but then, slowly, carefully, she lowers her arm, bends forward, and with the stretch and grace of a ballerina, she sets the object on the ground.

It glints in the early morning sunlight.

Not a bomb. Not a gun. Not a weapon.

A goblet.

I step back and raise my hands up in the air again. My teeth flash. My nose ring twinkles. I am grinning from ear to ear.

After that, they got me to lie down on my stomach with my arms stretched out from my sides; then, they moved in, and they cuffed me, and they took me away.

Left behind on the sidewalk where I had lain was the goblet, whose sunlit glint haloed the wet imprint of my body, winged and skirted, just like an angel in the snow.

POSTSCRIPT

Deacon Molene passed away on December 4, 2003, at the age of 97. He never regained consciousness. His wife, Emily, 96, followed him exactly one month later. Whether she was aware of her husband's death is unclear.

Dr. Phillips's precious collection had been returned to the safety of its glass case before the bomb went off, and the books and manuscripts in it were unharmed, although the famous display of his own work in all its translations and editions was pretty well destroyed.

A memorial fund was created in honor of the Molenes, designated to finance a renovation of the Molene House that will soon be home to the Springer College "Forevermore Library" where a special collection of rare books, manuscripts, and historically valuable archives will be kept and put safely on display. And as of this date, negotiations are currently in progress with a publisher who has expressed an interest in reprinting Forevermore.

John and Sarah Steele's baby girl was born on April 1, 2004. Her name is Rose.

Mollie Mifflin was charged with Criminal Trespass in the First Degree, a Class A misdemeanor that carries with it the maximum penalty of a year in prison and a $1,000 fine. But under pressure from the community and the college, those charges were eventually dropped and the case was dismissed.

A poem by Joyce (the Widow) Blanding appears in a recent issue of The New Yorker. It's entitled "A Marriage Made in Heaven," and in it, the poet describes a conversation between two unnamed people who have been married to each for many years. It's not until the last line of the poem that we understand that they are actually dead, but they seem to be very happy, wherever they are.

We notice that U.S.A. Today has reported what they've called a "freak accident" (but we know better) that occurred on October 12, 2009, where a microwave oven exploded in the kitchen of a home in Tampa, Florida, in what appears to have been a deliberate act of violence. No one was injured, but the police investigation of the crime revealed that the four young boys living in the house at the time had been systematically starved by their adoptive parents, Vernon and Ray-Anne Peterson. The Petersons each face multiple charges of child abuse, child neglect, reckless endangerment, and welfare fraud even as they continue to claim that their sons' scrawny bodies and brittle health stem from birth defects and eating disorders. Happily, all four boys have been placed in protective custody, where they have made remarkable gains in both weight and height since being removed from the home, and medical examinations show no evidence of disease or disorders.

As for the one remaining goblet, it was overlooked in the scuffle of Mollie's arrest, but Postscript managed to retrieve it from the sidewalk where she'd left it. It's in our possession now, and it's in a safe place. Its glass is still the flawless frosted swirl of smoky blue that it always was, but now its fluted bowl is supported by a stem that forms the perfectly formed bodies of a woman and a man, entwined. Our hope is that we'll find a use for it someday and that when we do, then your fondest wish is going come true.

About The Author

Susan Taylor Chehak is a graduate of the University of Iowa Writers' Workshop and the author of several novels, including *Smithereens*, *The Story of Annie D.*, and *Harmony*. Her short stories have appeared in Folio, Coe Review, Guernica Magazine, and The Adirondack Review, among other places. Her most recent publication is a work of nonfiction, *What Happened to Paula: The Anatomy of a True Crime*. Susan has taught fiction writing in the low residency MFA program at Antioch University, Los Angeles, the UCLA Extension Writers' Program, the University of Southern California, and the Summer Writing Festival at the University of Iowa. She grew up in Cedar Rapids, Iowa, spent many years in Los Angeles, lives occasionally in Toronto, and at present calls Colorado her home.

Website: http://www.susantaylorchehak.com
Twitter: http://twitter.com/stchehak
Facebook: http://www.facebook.com/stchehak
Blog: http://www.tumblr.com/blog/susantaylorchehak

Also By Susan Taylor Chehak

What Happened to Paula: The Anatomy of a True Crime

Rampage

Smithereens

Harmony

Dancing On Glass

The Story of Annie D.

Find more good books at
http://www.foreverlandpress.com

www.ingramcontent.com/pod-product-compliance
Lightning Source LLC
Chambersburg PA
CBHW060552260626
47161CB00003B/1166

* 9 7 8 0 9 9 6 0 4 0 8 3 9 *